Moving

Dedicated to my amazing wife, Jocelyn, even though she hates this sort of attention. Thank you for changing my life, for encouraging me to write a newspaper column, and for loving me so well. In you, God gave me more than I even knew to ask for – good thing He's smarter than I am! Sweetie, Precious, Cuddle Bunny – are you sick of the praise yet? Well, too stinkin' bad.

i

Comments about Kent Sipes' 1st book,
Thank You, my Friends – the 5-year Plan:

"*The finest book you could ever purchase on any subject. The author is a genius, and this book should be on the coffee table of every home in America, even those households that don't speak English!*" – Kent's Mama

"*Cute!*" – Kent's consulting co-worker, Fred

"*Please buy more copies! They're cheap!!*" - Jocelyn

"*It's a book! And I know the author!!* – Kent's Aunt Dorothy

To contact the author for private readings or speaking engagements, to order books in bulk, or to seek goat consultation (Don't get any — run while you can!!), feel free to send an e-mail message to: sipeskent@gmail.com.

My "hopeful pine" – the only transplant yet to survive in my front yard

Contents

Goodwill Cowboy Boots

(Note: this was supposed to be in the 1ˢᵗ volume – 'The 5-year Plan')

We're about to hold our 5ᵗʰ-annnual Health Fair – and the "we" keeps getting bigger. This year, it encompasses my church (Chandler 1ˢᵗ Assembly), 1ˢᵗ Methodist, and "The Baptist Behemoth" (Rock Hill – just kidding), plus the Catholic Church. My Pastor wants to involve as many churches as possible in the effort, so that we represent "the body of Christ", rather than just individual "tribes" of churches (though I dearly love mine!)

Getting ready to do this Health Fair reminds me of the 1ˢᵗ we did – it was a much more modest affair, in which we gave away backpacks of school supplies, provided some medical check-ups, handed out DQ Blizzard gift cards, and prayed over each kid. My then-fiancée, Jocelyn, helped me run a bounce house (We got married the following Saturday). At the time, I was a bit miffed at our assigned jobs – we both have Master's degrees; surely there was some better way we could help! But I reminded myself to be humble, we did what we were told, and we scoped out better assignments for the next year.

One kid I'll never forget from the 1st year was the 7-year-old boy who was reluctant to take off his cowboy boots to climb into the bounce house, because "My daddy gotten them for me at the Goodwill!". He was so proud of those worn-out boots that were at least 2 sizes too big for his feet, and I was amazed at how grateful a kid can be for something so humble. We both teared up, and resolved that we would be shoe-fitters the 2nd year, when we were going to start giving those away.

That year, I will always remember the little princess on whom I fitted pink, sparkly sneakers, and she proved how well they fit by dancing(!) away from my shoe station. I still tear up at that –

how could anyone <u>not</u> want a piece of that action?!? That was only one of the 700 pair we gave away; only one of the 700 kids we were privileged to bless.

Because, how often does one get the chance to do <u>exactly</u> what Jesus did in washing the feet of his disciples? We wipe stinky feet that have been tooling around in worn-out flip-flops or hand-me-down shoes of the wrong size – or in Goodwill cowboy boots. We put on clean socks, then measure each foot and send a shoe runner to bring back a couple of choices. We let the child choose the shoe, we try it on him/her, and we ask the kid to walk around in them, or, better yet, show us how fast he can run (or, if it's a little princess, maybe she'll dance!)

Even though I loved fitting shoes on munchkins (years 2 & 3), I get restless being confined to one place and waiting for the kids to come to me, so in the 4th year I invented my *own* job at the Health Fair – I became the "Welcomer". I walked the entire Health Fair, handing out water & snacks to the workers, giving breaks as needed, but mostly welcoming kids & their parents/grandparents to our event. I've never been in the position to have to wait in line for school supplies or shoes, and it must be tough on these adults. And I know that waiting in line is not a favorite activity for the kids!

So I try to meet each kid and (with the adult's permission) give him/her some candy, and tell everyone what to expect inside. I thank each family (nearly 1,500 people this year) for being part of our event, and I'll be handing out cold bottles of water to anyone in line who wants one, along with candy for the munchkins. My young Assistant, Kaleb (Yo, bud! Looking forward to hangin' with you again!), will pull a wagon filled with water and spare candy, tons of which I will carry in my cargo shorts, utility vest, and sun hat.

So, whether you're a worker, a donor (Thanks to Ace Hardware and Spartan Utilities, who handed me checks for the

Health Fair!), or one of the families we are <u>blessed</u> to serve, come be a part of this effort – even if it's just to see the chaos! OK, it's not <u>total</u> chaos – our Coordinator, Georgia, runs the craziness with a firm hand – but come check it out.

You might even get to see a princess dance in pink, sparkly shoes!

The main floor of our 2019 Health Fair

I replaced some rotten boards on my porch... then I had to paint them... then I had to paint the old boards... then the steps... then the handrails... and the pillars... and the door frame... and the windows...and the porch swing...

Manly, Yes, but I Like it, Too!

Several years ago I was in charge of Training for a construction tool sales group, which regularly held a "Tool School", in which salespeople learned to sell power tools more effectively, and got hands-on experience with lots of equipment. As someone with almost no construction skills (I injured myself **every day** while working in home construction for a week), I still found my first experience with this to be loads of fun! I got to cut apart a car hood with an abrasive disc, slice concrete with a water-cooled saw, and fire nails into concrete with a powder-actuated tool (PAT).

I often felt the need to grunt in a manly way during that and subsequent Tool Schools. And I sometimes miss using some of those tools. As I passed a young guy running a small backhoe last week, I thought of a buddy of mine who, years ago, took a job with Dallas County on a Dallas County road crew. He had previously managed a Radio Shack, and this seemed to me to be a step down, professionally.

Then I found out that he earned more money working for the County, with almost no pressure, and that he was learning to operate heavy equipment. I became a jealous man. My retail "management" job was full of pressure (to make the books balance) and boredom (as we waited for customers to enter). Suddenly, the road crew seemed like an amazing "guy" situation.

Both of my regular readers will remember my fervent desire to own a tractor ('Tractor Lust'), but that desire is rooted in what I could do with the *attachments* – mow brush, dig holes, push dirt around, and (with a big enough tractor) pull stumps – guy stuff. I remember a story I read years ago about a jackhammer operator who typically had an audience of several suit-and-tie-clad professionals while he pounded apart concrete at a downtown intersection. Then one day, one of them asked if he could take a turn running the jackhammer.

The operator was a bit confused by the request, but decided it would be OK, as long as "suit guy" put on safety glasses (and the foreman wasn't around). So, the office worker handed over his jacket, rolled up his shirt sleeves, and happily pounded concrete for 15 minutes, at which time another office worker (from the line that quickly formed) took over. The jackhammer operator began charging to run the tool, and made $60 per hour above what he was already being paid by the construction company. The office workers got to play with a "big-boy toy", work out their frustrations, and loosen their back & shoulder muscles.

So, I plan to create a theme park called "Man Zone", in which men get to use jackhammers, concrete saws, and PATs, plus front-end loaders, backhoes, bulldozers, and road rollers. Yes, I realize that some of this equipment is very costly, but even the big vehicles are less pricey than a new roller coaster. And some of the cost could be defrayed by the large tool companies, who would certainly pay the park to exclusively use their PATs or concrete saws.

Women would be barred from the park, because they just can't appreciate the value of "guy" activities (such as communicating via loud burps). Yes, I realize that banning women will make them angry – the Promise Keepers conferences faced this same issue for years, but we didn't fight to attend women's conferences! Men need time with just men, to do manly things, like grunting, spitting, and competing in meaningless contests.

There will also be a section called "Logger Land", where men could don long spikes ("gaffes") and race to the top of poles, fell trees with 24" chain saws, and roll logs in a simulated river. Two-man teams would compete to cut through 6'- thick timber using tandem saws.

In the section called "Kill Zone", especially brave men, equipped only with bows and arrows, would hunt wild boars, to give the boars a fighting chance. Both men and boars would be fenced in, and no man will be allowed leave the Kill Zone unless he is carrying a boar's head. (Yes, some men would die, and No, we are not accepting any men volunteered by their wives.)

Restaurants in the park would hold buckwheat pancake-eating contests in which the loser has to pay for all the cakes and coffee both men consume (because it's no fun if there's nothing at stake!). Other snack bars would sell habañeros, scorpion peppers, and ghost chiles. The first man to eat three of each without passing out, screaming, or tearing out his own midsection would be the winner. Paramedics would be standing by with ice cream.

Days at the park would begin at 6 AM, when gates open to all men willing to pay the $100 entry fee, and every man would be required to compete at least once every two hours. Men who lose three contests would be expelled from the park, until there are only a dozen left, who would be awarded t-shirts that read "Yes, I **am** Superior". Any man who manages to sneak back into the park after being expelled would be allowed to stay, because many men consider "sneakiness" a virtue (not me - I'm not smart enough to be a good sneak).

We'll need "Father & Son" competitions too, in which dads and sons could compete against other dads and sons. But no man gets thrown out for losing these contests, because any man who competes with his son is a winner. And any dad who shows up with a boy who's not his own, because that boy's birth father isn't involved in his life, automatically gets a "Superior" t-shirt – because he is.

During unemployment, I did lots of painting

13

Disaster Camping

Camping - I used to love it, before I discovered just <u>how</u> <u>much</u> I enjoy air conditioning. When I was 8 years old, my parents let me set up a pup tent in the back yard, where a buddy and I braved the outdoors of our unfenced lawn until rain and wind collapsed our tent around us. When I got a bit older, I would join my big brother camping on Marathon Oil property a couple of blocks behind our home. It wasn't quite "wilderness", but it was camping.

In fact, the "backyard camping" theme has been in my mind for a few years – I'm clearing a space in our acre of woods where parents from our church can bring young kids to safely introduce them to camping in the woods, only 50' from our house. None of our structures are visible through the trees, so the kids could feel like they were in the wilderness, but would be close enough to the house that we could help with any camping disaster.

And I <u>know</u> camping disasters. I've written about taking a group of church guys, aged 8-14, camping at a nature preserve on the edge of our suburban town, for the purpose of teaching them "fire safety". After getting the boys into their tents, I struggled out of my jeans preparatory to climbing into my own tiny pup tent (there wasn't room inside to shed my jeans).

Unfortunately, I tripped over my size-11 feet, and very sloooooowly tilted toward the last burning embers of my campfire. I was faced with the choice of allowing my entire left side to kiss the coals, or putting my hand down on one to arrest my fall. So I deliberately put my right hand on a red-hot coal and pushed off. "Ouch" doesn't really express my feelings at the time, but I never learned to cuss, so only a faint <u>scream</u> came from my throat.

As I iced my 2nd-degree burns, my two assistants, 20-somethings like myself (but even <u>less</u> responsible), debated about how to transport me to the ER. The younger one proposed to smash through the park gate (locked to prevent unauthorized entry after dark) with his 1970s muscle car - this guy had watched too many 'Dukes of Hazzard' episodes. His older brother was slightly more sensible, and suggested that we visit the resident Park Host to request that he open the gate for us.

After treatment in the ER, I was sent home for the night. My cohorts were responsible for breaking down our campsite and transporting the church's tents and other camping gear back to church. Their approach to this was to cram all the wet, dirty gear into the trunk of the muscle car, and deliver it to the church the next day. It was crammed into a large closet, where it mildewed for a few weeks until I had healed sufficiently to spend a day allowing it to dry outside.

Camping with others from my church was a common theme throughout my life. My first "non-family" campout was with a group of Royal Rangers – this was a church program modeled on the Boy Scouts program, but with more of a spiritual emphasis. I was thrilled to go on our first group camping trip to Red Hills State Park, about 20 minutes from our rural Illinois community, especially since I would get to use all my official Royal Ranger outdoor gear (mostly paid for by my big brother - see my 'Super Sipes' article).

Everything was fine until the parents showed up to see our campsite and get an idea of what we were learning. I immediately communicated to my parents that I had learned their 8-year-old boy would be very happy to return with them to sleep in the safety of his own bed. They responded by assuring me that everything would be fine, to which I in turn responded by assuring them that I would be eaten by bears during the night.

Later that night, having heard no bears approach our roadside campsite for a few hours, I settled in to "enjoying nature". I finally drifted off to sleep, and awakened the next morning to stumble out of my tent and burn my own breakfast in my "Official Royal Ranger Camp Skillet". I'm happy to report that I have not been eaten by bears in over 50 years of camping, though at times my personal odor might have proven attractive to them.

It was usually me who instigated camping trips with church friends. Every few months, especially during the cooler months, I would get sick of all the concrete and buildings of our Dallas-area suburb and decide that I had to get away for at least a night. If I didn't have time to travel as far as Tyler State Park, we would head to a Dallas city park on the edge of town – at least the 40 acres of trees there didn't smell like the city, though highway traffic noise was a constant backdrop.

I must have been all of 14 years old when a group of men from my church decided to try camping at Lake Lavon in late January, as part of our Royal Ranger group, a version of the Boy Scouts customized for our denomination. I'm not quite sure who thought camping in January sounded like a good idea – I don't think any of them were stupid enough to listen to *me* – but that means an <u>actual</u> <u>adult</u> thought it was wise to camp beside a lake when the forecast temperature was in the mid-20s.

Besides me, our Youth Leader and two older church members braved the cold. I was the only actual Royal Ranger, and I believe I also had the most camping experience of the group. One of the men had never before been camping, and was somehow talked into this foolishness - what an introduction to the great outdoors!

After setting up camp and building a fire, we huddled around it to thaw our hands. This was necessary every few minutes to keep them from becoming too numb to use. As we began to cook dinner, Ken (one of our deacons) noted that a little BBQ sauce in the beans would be good, so we deduced that a <u>lot</u> of BBQ sauce in the beans would be <u>excellent</u> – and we were waaaaaay off.

In fact, they were barely edible – but, on a positive note, they warmed us up (then and later!).

Normally, a cold night would mean we manly males would squat around the campfire, telling stories such as "I once had this girlfriend who hugged like a bear… Come to think of it, she looked like one, too!". But, this being a church-sponsored event, Ken gave a short devotional – something about God and nature, I think. It was a bit hard to make out the words through his shivering.

Then we sang a worship chorus (either 'How Great Thou Art' or 'Blessed Assurance' – again, it was hard to pick out the words, especially since I had my hands over my ears half of the time, to prevent frostbite). We didn't care to hang around the fire any longer after that (having run out of hot coffee to pour on our hands) so each of us retired to his tent by 9 PM.

We had a primo camping spot <u>right</u> at the water's edge, close enough to feel the bitterly cold wind blasting unhindered through our tents. I tried to attach a thick trash bag against the outside of mine as a windbreak, but it kept blowing away, and I finally gave up chasing it down (What's the statute of limitations on littering?).

I had brought sweats to wear to bed, and I also put on two pairs of socks and a toboggan cap. But even inside my sleeping bag, I shivered so violently that I could not sleep, so I gathered the clothes I'd been wearing and put them on over the sweats. I was still too cold to sleep, so I pulled from my duffel bag the clothes I planned to wear the *next* day and struggled to fasten on that set as an additional layer of insulation.

Finally, around midnight, I got to sleep, but I kept hearing a car periodically turn over. The next morning, I found out that Ken, our first-time camper, spent most of the night in the car. He would start the engine and turn on the heater until the car got warm, at which point he'd turn off the engine and go to sleep. When the car became too cold again, he would repeat the process. This went on until breakfast.

...Which was pretty bleak, since we could find no more deadfalls for firewood, and an icy mist was falling. Tony chopped down a small tree with the brand-new hatchet he'd brought along (risking a hefty fine), but we had a tough time building a fire with the green wood, especially since our charcoal lighter fluid was running low. We finally got a tiny fire built and Harland (the other adult responsible for this fiasco) cooked some sausage and scrambled eggs, which we washed down with truly <u>horrible</u> instant coffee – the orange juice had frozen solid.

We packed up and headed back to civilization, and our exploits were included in the next church bulletin, with the caption: 'Royal Ranger Campout – a Success?'. I've never again tried camping in January, which once and for all answers the question my nephew, Keith, once asked me: "Can you *learn*?!?".

...But not that <u>well</u> - I did another cold campout in my early 20s, with two guys from my church who were gullible enough to go along with my wild idea – this time, in November. I had spotted a beautiful campsite overlooking a cove at Lake Texoma – unfortunately, this campsite was booked solid... until Winter.

I conned two of my friends into making the trip – apparently, I was an effective salesman. We set up camp as the clouds gathered, and I managed to roast smoked sausage for dinner. As we were sitting around the campfire, the rain began to fall, and became a deluge.

No problem – we were <u>men</u> (Ha!) We could handle the cold... the rain... darkness at 7 PM... the boredom. We three huddled in a two-man tent, trying not to press against the canvas and let the rain in. Hanging from the tent post was a small battery-powered lantern, which we used to attempt to play cards for about 30 minutes. Then we gave up and ran to our individual tents to attempt sleep.

The icy rain fell hard all night. When we awakened the next morning, the rain had slackened off a bit, but our fire was out, all our firewood was soaked, and we decided to simply break camp as quickly as possible. We stuffed the tents and sleeping bags in the trunk, but kept the ice chest with all our food beside me in the back seat. We headed out of the state park toward the closest convenience store – our goals were hot coffee, hot food, and a dry environment.

Though the heater was cranked to maximum, we were all shivering uncontrollably. My solution was to insert as many calories into my mouth as possible.

The bread was soaked, so I rolled up slices of lunchmeat, chewing them as quickly as possible before swallowing. After that was gone, we hit the eggs we'd brought along for breakfast – raw, just like Rocky.

I was responsible for pouring the milk and orange juice into plastic cups, because we still weren't <u>quite</u> barbaric enough to drink directly from the jugs. We all laughed at how miserable we were, though a laugh mixed with shivering is a <u>really</u> creepy sound.

The 25-minute drive to the convenience store seemed so long... Once we arrived at the Promised Land, or <u>whatever</u> the store was called, I went straight for the coffee pot, then found a breakfast biscuit containing a slab of egg, greasy sausage, and cheese. After dousing it liberally with Tabasco® sauce, I barely managed to pay the cashier before adding it and a cinnamon roll to the <u>massive</u> amount of calories I'd already consumed.

When I finally felt warm, about 20 minutes later, I fell asleep. I don't remember much of the drive home, but I <u>do</u> remember that when we arrived, both of them blamed <u>me</u>

for the entire ordeal... as if I could talk
them into camping in the middle of Winter!

Stark terror

A couple of my "young friends" from waaaay back – they probably have their own kids by now! Oh, and I'm wearing another of my t-shirt designs.

BB Rifleman

Some readers might remember the black &
white TV western called 'The Rifleman'. I
watched the show, when Bonanza reruns
weren't being broadcast. Of course, this
was
"back in the day" when we only had 7-8 TV
channels that really came in clearly, so
choices weren't plentiful. 'The Rifleman' was
about a farmer who just wanted to be left
alone, but was frequently called upon to
use his skills with a firearm to protect
something or other. The show also had
many father/son moments in which the
Rifleman's son, "Mark" learned some
important life lesson (such as how to
effectively shoot someone, once all non-
violent options had been exhausted).

My dad gave me opportunities to learn to
be a "straight shooter", but most of those
were as part of our few hunting excursions,
which I didn't enjoy. I suppose I didn't have
the patience to sit in a duck blind or deer
stand, flush quail, or nail squirrels to a
branch. These trips also took away from my
reading time. Now that I'm older, I still
don't hunt (or fish, as I mentioned in

Hunting? Fishing? Nah..., but I can certainly appreciate the peaceful stillness of an early-morning hunt, and a friend from church recently gave us some wonderful deer sausage (which I added to some red beans & rice).

We own a handgun, for last-ditch protection, but our most handy weapon is a BB rifle we bought to scare off roaming dogs who might hurt our chickens. After being nailed in the butt with a BB, a dog just leaves our property alone. And we occasionally have to deal with other hazards – snakes and possums have eaten eggs and tried to kill chickens. I've dispatched more than one snake to wherever snakes go when they die (my Pastor says they're all sent from Hell), and the possums became well-acquainted with my yard rake.

If I tried to use the handgun on either of the above-mentioned pests, it's likely I would hit anything *but* the intended animal – my aim is that poor! I once tried to knock a soda can from atop a fence by shooting at it from 12 feet away – no luck. Then I moved to 10 feet away, then 8 feet, 6 feet, 4 feet... I finally managed to hit the can when I was within 3 feet of it. I can shoot OK with a rifle, but I doubt a snake or possum would wait long enough for me to sight down the barrel and squeeze off a shot – and I'd probably have to be inside the chicken house, and therefore shooting from a maximum of 5 feet away.

Our church now has an armed Security team, and its members communicate via radios & earpieces. I'm confident that any of them (some ex-military) could take down a threat to the safety of our congregation, if needed. In fact, a fellow believer I encountered at the gym told me that, if an armed assailant tried to cause a problem in his Cowboy Church, the last sound that person would hear would be the cocking of 50 handguns.

Of course, I hate that we have to even consider self-defense in church. But, at least in this area, churches are not "soft targets". Not to get political, but I've wondered if we should arm school janitors for the same reason. I wonder how they'd react?

Maybe a kid would hear this: "Did you mean to drop that candy wrapper? Think very carefully before you answer, punk. Would you like to slowly bend over and pick it up? I thought so. And here are a few paper towels to clean up that puddle at your feet."

Or, what if we armed Assistant Principals (typically responsible for discipline) – maybe a kid would hear: "So, you brought a knife to school? Didn't your mama teach you never to bring a knife to a gunfight?". The 357 Magnum could hang right next to the paddle (with holes in it to lessen wind resistance – the paddle, not the handgun), as an added "encouragement" to follow the rules.

Due to some recent gun scares, my wife has informed me that we need to both become proficient in the use of our handgun, and earn our "Concealed Carry" permits. She'll probably score better than me on target practice, but then, so would anyone who's not legally blind. I just hope I don't accidentally shoot our firearms instructor, as I aim for a target downrange.

Now, I must do some research. I've promised our church Security Team leader that I'll put together some scenarios for his next training session, and I've volunteered to be the "disturbed person" who needs to be escorted out of the sanctuary. My plan is to avoid overplaying my part, so no one feels the need to wrestle me to the ground. Heaven forbid someone should need to draw his gun – I'd probably make a little puddle (piddle?) on the sanctuary carpet.

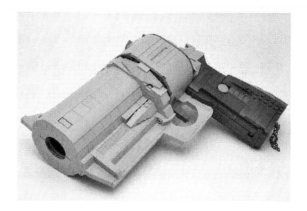

*Reunited with my buddy, Josh, in Orlando –
and I show up looking as if he'd brought me
in off the street for a hot meal!!*

45 More to Go...

This week, the fabulous Jocelyn and I will celebrate five years of marriage. Since the appropriate gift for a 5th anniversary is supposed to be something having to do with "paper", I decided to commemorate it with... an article in the newspaper. Because I found this wonderful lady relatively late in life, I've always asked God for at least 50 years with her. That would mean I'll live to be 102, but, hey, 50 years doesn't seem nearly enough. My parents made almost 60 years together – Dad died a few weeks too early.

I've written about her before, and she'll likely be embarrassed by this column, just as she was by others directed at her (see *Light the Corners of my Mind*; *I Work For the Queen; In All the Wrong Places*). In fact, she may be a bit miffed at me for writing this. However, she <u>is</u> allowing me to dedicate my 2nd collection of columns to her (Purt, my overgrown puppy, was the 2nd choice). *Thank You, my Friends – How Did This Happen?!?* will be available on Amazon sometime this Fall.

If you happen to like this column, get a few laughs from it, maybe gain some insight, or even tear up with me (see my article *Blubbering Idiot*), it's all <u>her</u> fault. I'd been writing for years for trade magazines, my consulting firm's newsletter, and LinkedIn – but I felt stifled by my narrow audience and subject matter. She "encouraged" me for months to submit some articles to our local paper, and I finally did. This column is now published in 6 East TX newspapers, and is read by up to 30,000 folks, in 19 states and 3 foreign countries – (thank you, ma'am, and PTL!).

More importantly, being Jocelyn's husband has made me a stronger, more confident man. And though I really hope I get 50 years with her, if I died tomorrow, I'd know I had been <u>well</u> <u>loved</u>. The fact that she made me stop using gasoline to burn up brush on our property has probably delayed my untimely death (see my article *Burning Down the House*). Diesel isn't as much fun, but it does allow me to keep my eyebrows and moustache.

Early on in our courtship, she asked me if I was "for real" – apparently, other men she had dated made a show of following Jesus, but had serious holes in their integrity. I

hope she still believes I am "for real" –
she's certainly had time to see the holes in
my integrity. I had to give up trying to be
her Superman during our first year together
– as much as I'd like to, I can't solve all her
problems.

I'm not her Source, anyway – she knows
that God is our true source. I love to give
her things, but I'm just the conduit. And
she's anything but selfish – for instance,
though she'd much rather make every
vacation a beach blitz, our last getaway was
to something more to my taste (hills and
trees). We rented a log cabin in Northern
Arkansas and rafted on the Buffalo River,
and we both loved it!.

Last year, we rented a 3-bedroom beach
house in Florida. We biked along the
shoreline, swam, dozed on the beach, and
ate picnic lunches. When we tired of the
sand and outdoors, we napped, read novels
(she got me interested in the *Jack Reacher*
series), and went out to dinner. After the
2nd day, I was tired of having sand in every
crevice of my body, but my sweetie loves
the beach, sun, and surf, so... I'm learning
to deal with the sand.

I'm not sure I'll <u>ever</u> be able to coax her into learning to snow ski (I love snowy peaks), since we're both firmly in middle age (Shhh!!! Don't tell her!). My plan has been to learn snowboarding at the same time she's taking skiing lessons, so that we're both "newbies" at our downhill sports, and we can cruise down the Beginner slopes together. Of course, the fact that I haven't been on a pair of skis in 30 years (40 pounds ago) might relegate me to newbie status <u>without</u> adding snowboarding.

Besides being a patient, wise mama to two kids (both adults now), Jocelyn helps lots of people deal with life's challenges, in her private practice (Back Porch Therapy). And after five years, I can sometimes tell when she's doing therapy on <u>me</u>. When talking to her, I'm sometimes reminded of a T-shirt for social workers that reads: "Keep talking, I'm diagnosing you!". And I've learned that when she asks "if we should maybe" take a specific course of action, she's not <u>really</u> asking – we'll probably end up doing whatever she mentioned.

She's a regular on our church's worship team, manages more than 20 chickens, keeps a garden (I get to cook with fresh vegetables and herbs), and is developing into a wonderful presenter. She's fiercely loyal to her family and devoted to her friends. And she's learned to cut off unhealthy relationships and foster close, reciprocating ones. I am immensely proud of her, and awed that I get to be her partner.

To say I love this woman doesn't go nearly far enough. One of the benefits to no longer being "on the road" for my job is that I get to demonstrate how much I care for her, in tangible ways. For me, that means cooking her breakfast and delivering it to the bed (she sometimes wakes up slooooowly) or the bathroom (where she's getting ready).

Jocelyn, I'm sorry if this embarrasses you, but you know me – I stink at keeping my feelings in, and I'm not shy. I've thanked you many times for marrying me, but here it is again. Thanks for being brave enough to let me into your life, thanks for not fleeing my house when I closed the blinds on our 3rd date, and thanks for giving me a "hope transfusion" five years ago.

Finally, thanks in advance for not sending me to sleep with the chickens because I wrote about you... again. I love you muchly, my CB.

"No, Kent – we <u>can't</u> bring any of these home to live in our pool!"

I'm a Travelin' Man...

Nearly 10 years ago, I became a professional traveler. I took the skills I had learned about teaching university staffers how to use a particular Oracle computer system "on the road". I immediately doubled my salary, and added a huge amount of job stress. My university job was very relaxed – I could take a long lunch hour (for racquetball or weightlifting at the SRC), and make it up on another day... or not.

The job stress I added somewhat counteracted the relationship stress I previously experienced when I got back from the university job, since I wasn't at home as often. And it replaced my ex's complaint that I didn't "earn enough to pay for us to have a child" with the complaint that I was "cocky about how much I made". In fact, my absence probably preserved our toxic marriage (for better or worse).

We learned a new routine when I was on the road, and became more "roomies" than spouses. Soon, the only living being happy to see me arrive home was my dog, Brindle (whom she kept in the divorce – don't get me started on that!). After she filed, and I moved to East Texas, my first trip for work scared me – I didn't know how I'd handle coming home to an empty house.

My kind neighbors Dona and Scooter took care of that, decorating my little house with more Christmas stuff than I'd ever seen in that amount of square feet. They also left a nice note, and some Christmas cookies to boot. I don't think I've ever been so overwhelmed! (Yes, of course I cried.)

My sweetie of five years has also learned a routine when I'm gone, but she's much happier to pick me up at the airport. Our son even remarked to her that, when I'm gone, "food doesn't magically appear in the fridge or on the dinner table". And we have another routine for when I'm "off the road", in which I try to take care of many more things around the house. I also try to stay out of my wife's way, which is much easier now that my home office is upstairs in our farmhouse.

Of course, this means that I'm likely to be in our son's way instead, since he previously had the entire 2nd floor to himself. He has already made the request that I not "blast my music" from the office.

I keep hoping that if I play Petra at a high-enough volume level, he'll come to appreciate their musical genius. These kids today, whatcha gonna do with them?...

I remember exactly where I was when I first saw this album cover!

Possibly the "Father" of Christian Rock –
Larry Norman – around 1972

Smack! "Yes, Sir?"

For the past several years, my Bible study routine has been to read a chapter or two every day, from three different sections of the Bible. I split up the sections into 1 OT history/prophecy book, 1 OT poetry book, and 1 NT book. So, on Monday morning, I might study from Jeremiah, on Tuesday from Psalms, and on Wednesday from Colossians. That way, I'm never JUST reading, say, Deuteronomy for a whole month, nor do I just get another Psalm every day.

It's a "complete Bible diet". I've used the same plan to read through my Bible several times in the past few years, and it's been a good plan – I even mixed it up this time by working backward through the NT and OT. For instance, I began by reading in Revelations, Song of Solomon, and Malachi. I read each book in normal chapter order, though.

Reading through the Bible gives me a "balanced diet" spiritually, but it's also raised some questions and caused some observations in my mind, like:

1. Does Jeremiah <u>ever</u> end?!? (Yes, but it's followed by Lamentations…)
2. Man, those Old-Testament people did a lot of "begatting"!
3. Bible folks, even the heroes, had the same flaws we do.
4. David (writer of Psalms) had a lot of the same questions I do.
5. New-Testament churches were far from perfect.
6. Folks who don't think the Bible is ever funny haven't read enough of it.
7. The Old and New Testaments are linked like tree branches and roots.
8. I will <u>never</u> learn everything the Bible has to teach me.
9. In Genesis, it doesn't take long for us to mess up things very badly.
10. The Bible is full of <u>really</u> good news and <u>really</u> bad news. But at the end of the Book (Revelations), everything wraps up in a really amazing way for those on the right side.

Purt, my big puppy, doesn't read the Bible, but he has taken in a good bit of it. When he was still teething, he ate a whole book out of my Grandmother's Bible – most of Leviticus. I've read that dogs don't really have a conception of cause & effect, so I couldn't smack him for what he'd done – he would have no idea of <u>why</u> I was swatting his butt.

And I don't always swat him there, either – this dog is amazingly stubborn (or really stupid, but I prefer to think it's just stubbornness). Smacking him on the hind end doesn't always get his attention, so I occasionally knock him on the head to get his attention. I think it's much the same as how God deals with me. I'm either thick or really stubborn, because I sometimes feel as if He's had to remind me forcefully of things I need to understand.

Purt and I had a "discussion" of this sort just recently. I had seasoned 8 round steaks, which I planned to broil just before my wife got home. I went to my closet, in the back half of our farmhouse, to change into my "yard-work" clothes. When I came back to the kitchen, I saw, on the floor, the paper towels that had covered the round steak, and, on the counter, an empty plate.

It had just happened (Purt is apparently a speed-eater), so I "reminded" him pretty strongly that he was not to put his paws on the kitchen counter and eat from our plates! And he's no quicker learner than I am, because this was not the first time he's gotten food off the counter. He devoured an entire Ribeye steak (see my column 'Ribeye Friends') recently.

But he learns no more slowly than I do. When the lovely Jocelyn and I had been dating for about a month, I was out on the riding mower, talking to God about her. I'm a pretty emotional guy, and I had to make sure I wasn't letting my emotions run away with me, so I asked Him if I was going the right way in this blossoming relationship.

He hit me so hard with the conviction that I needed to snag this woman as quickly as possible that I compare it to being smacked upside the head with a 2x4. He did the same thing when He convinced (Ha!) me that I was supposed to start working with our Kid's Ministry on Wednesday nights – here's how the conversation went:

"Hey, Kent! That need for adults to listen to the kids recite their memory verses? That's where I want you – now."

"Hey, God – is this really you? Because I like sitting in this Bible Study with my sweetie every Wednesday night."

"Hey, Kent (**Smack!!**) - how many times do I have to repeat myself?"

"Hey, God – at least once more, maybe twice."

"Hey, Kent (**Smack**, **Smack**!!) – is your head still ringing? Got it yet?"

"Yes, sir, God – kids, verses – I'm your man. Sure this is where you want me? Uh, never mind, I'll volunteer as soon as the lights stop flashing in my brain."

Many years ago, one of my nephews asked me, "Can you <u>learn</u>?!?". The answer is yes... just not right away.

At Crawford's Cabins in Jasper, AR – put your feet up for some light reading...

No Nothing

Warning - Time for another rant.
There's a great evil out there that needs to
be eradicated: yes, I'm talking about the
Cleveland Browns. In an age of marketing
(in which Jerry Jones purchased the
Cowboys for $115 million; now worth over
$2 billion), the Browns use no logo on their
helmets or jerseys. They're consistently
near the bottom of NFL merchandise sales,
because – what do they have to to sell but
"orange"?

The Cleveland Browns' helmets are plain
orange, like the color of OJ gone bad. In
fact, the person for whom the team was
named (Paul Brown) once owned two
teams with plain, stark helmets. In the early
days of the NFL, he also started the
Cincinnati Bengals – when the NFL told Mr.
Brown that he couldn't have two teams with
identical orange helmets, he reluctantly had
a **B** added to each side of the Bengals
helmets (now they have really cool tiger-
striped helmets).

The NFL had a chance to get rid of the Browns when the original team moved to Baltimore (and changed its name to the Ravens – more on that later). After a few years, the NFL expanded again and Cleveland got another NFL franchise, but the city had learned its lesson, and came up with a tough, cool team name and emblem –

HA! Nope, they said, "Why no, we <u>can't</u> learn! Let's call our new team The Browns!".

And Browns fans are <u>devoted</u>. One example: the Director of the boy's home where I served in the late 1980s was a die-hard Browns devotee, so much that, when he invited me to watch a Cowboys – Browns game (on a TV set that I gave him), I was not allowed to cheer for the Cowboys. We didn't hang out any more that evening.

And the Browns are just the <u>worst</u> example of wasted helmet space. I was remarking to a co-worker who's devoted to the New Orleans Saints that I just couldn't get excited about a team with a flower on its helmets, and he asked me, seriously, "Hey, what do you have against the Holy Trinity?!?". Apparently, the fleur-de-lis is supposed to represent the Trinity.

But my point was that they could have done something really cool for their emblem, like an angel with a flaming sword – because true saints (Jesus followers) really are **powerful**.

There are some other awful team logos out there:

- The Packers, named for the meat-packing industry that was big in Green Bay when the team was formed

- The Steelers, who use the old US Steel emblem, only on one side of each helmet.

- The Dolphins – come on - Flipper? Does anybody think that's tough or intimidating?

- The Ravens – this team name & emblem were obviously chosen by a committee, because no individual would pick what is, in essence, a vulture. The name is supposed to be a reference to Edgar Allen Poe, who, apparently, lived in the area when he wrote his poem, *The Raven*.

- The Bears, who once used a pretty cool bear's head on either side of their helmets, but now just use a stylized letter **C**.

- The Arizona Cardinals, who use the head of this robin-sized bird as their emblem. Has a cardinal <u>ever</u> struck fear in anyone's heart? This team used to be in St. Louis, and shared the name with the baseball Cardinals - they didn't bother to change the name when the team was transplanted to Phoenix. But the name doesn't fit the environment - has a wild cardinal ever been <u>seen</u> in Arizona?

- SF 49ers and NY Giants – a "49" and an "NY". 'Nuff said.

If I haven't yet offended your particular fan sensibilities (I know that East TX has a lot of Saints fans), feel free to contact me, after which I'll be happy to find some problem with the name, emblem, and/or color scheme of your favorite team. Because, hey, why waste a good rant?

*This has been a rant. Had this been an genuine emergency, you would have been instructed to actually pay attention. It's now safe to be around me without fear of offence - Mostly *

*And don't even get me started on the NBA!

The name of Jocelyn's therapy practice came from... our back porch, of course!

Ribeye Friends

I've mentioned previously that in my travels (mostly for work), I most value the <u>people</u> I meet. On a recent hop from Tyler to DFW, I chatted with my seatmate, an oilfield worker who regularly commutes to/from Saudi Arabia to train & manage local oilfield workers. He's there for two months, then home for two months, and has done so for years.

Since he's gone for so long, he refuses to give up at least one "comfort food" – bacon. Of course, the importation of pork products into that country is illegal (because of Sharia law), so he simply tells the Saudi immigration inspectors that it's beef jerky – they don't know the difference.

He also told me quite a bit about raising cattle during our 25-minute flight, and that cheaper cattle breeds still produce a good steak. Then he told me he had three levels of friends: "Burger", "Sirloin", and "Ribeye". Casual acquaintances and distant family who come to his house for dinner are fed home-grown burgers, and closer friends/family receive sirloin steaks. His "homies" get ribeyes.

And he expects that his closest friends will reciprocate by only feeding him ribeyes when he's a guest at their homes. He told me that he once refused to eat a burger offered him at a "Ribeye" friends home – he was very offended, and told his host to bring him a ribeye. Well, I'm not about to object when a friend feeds me, unless it involves liver, asparagus, beets, or cantaloupe. I don't eat other organ meats, like lengua, but my (mostly Gringo) friends aren't likely to offer me that Mexican specialty.

I can understand offering different folks different levels of food, though. If my Pastor and his wife come for dinner, I'm probably going to offer them the best food I can, but if it's one of "my munchkins" and his/her parent/grandparent has brought the kid over to swim in our pool... I'm probably grilling hot dogs. A couple well from church whom we know pretty well might get something in between (I do a truly beautiful BBQ Chicken).

Apparently, Purt (my overgrown Giant Schnauzer puppy) thinks he's a "Ribeye friend". Steaks, especially ribeyes, aren't common in our household right now, due to my unemployment and our family's new "clean eating" emphasis, but I have been cleaning out the big freezer and recently cooked some steaks I'd had stashed away for a "Pastor dinner" that never happened. I broiled two ribeyes and a huge t-bone for our family of three (the boy's home from college for the summer).

After giving the filet from the t-bone to my lovely bride, and giving Ben the rest of that steak, I cut a reasonable chunk for myself from one of the ribeyes, then pushed the baking sheet toward the back of the counter to prevent Purt from being overcome by temptation. When I returned to the kitchen later to clean up the mess I'd left from cooking dinner, zero leftover steak remained on the baking sheet.

Since nothing else on the counter was disturbed, and even the outline of the steaks in congealed fat was still visible on the aluminum foil, I decided that Ben must have <u>really</u> liked the steaks and decided that a second helping of 1½ ribeyes was justified. Usually, when Purt steals our food, he does a more complete job of it. But my wife assured me that even our 6' 2" 19-year-old couldn't be that hungry – <u>my</u> <u>dog</u> was the culprit.

And, while it's true that Purt and I have a special friendship (he's my "big buddy"), we're **not** "Ribeye Friends". He and my wife's Boston Terrier, Ranger, get plenty of steak fat, gristle, chicken skin, bacon grease, and the occasional slippery hot dog, but not their own steaks. And Purt certainly didn't offer **me** any part of the two ribeyes he stole – even the gristle. But maybe that's why he left the fat outline on the cookie sheet – he figured that was enough to share with his "big buddy".

I object – Purt's not even treating me like a "burger friend". But considering levels of friendship makes me think about how important I am in the lives of the people around me – I want to be a "Ribeye Friend" with more of them, regardless of what we feed each other. I want to be involved in their real lives, ask real questions about how they're doing, and be truly open about what's going on in mine.

Somehow, I just don't think Purt and I will reach that level of friendship – we have communication issues. I do talk to him (my side of the conversation usually involves some form of the word "No!"), and he tries to talk to me, using barks or a quizzical, quiet sort of howl. He becomes very confused when I use his own language back at him – if I bark at him, he doesn't know what to do with the input.

I wonder if there are "Dog Food" levels of friendship? We feed Purt from a big bag that costs over $40 at Tractor Supply. Yep, that's love, alright.

And he almost <u>never</u> eats anyone!!

Never. Again.

Not that Deep

Deep truths. Remarkable insights. I'd love to write about those, but, apparently, I've been assigned to the "Humor" section. Don't get me wrong – I love to laugh, and to share the laughs with y'all.

But, occasionally, I have a serious thought about scripture, politics, life lessons, or some other important topic. My kind editors print nearly everything I submit, but I'm following a Divine directive to "target the funny". Yes, I'm on a mission from God. Now, for those of you who have never *noticed* any humor in my writing, please notice that I said "target" – humor has been my goal, and I'm sure I haven't always achieved it.

My guess is that there are plenty of other writers who do a much better job than I of plumbing "deep" topics or conservative political thought. I, on the other hand, get hate mail when simply mentioning how funny I thought it was that liberals and conservatives both called for an NFL boycott (for opposite reasons). By the way, since I gave up watching the NFL during the National Anthem protests, I just haven't

cared enough to take up the habit again –
I'd rather nap on Sunday afternoons, or
watch something with my wife on a Monday
evening.

So, from me, you get to hear about funny
things my munchkins have said to me
recently (or stupid things I've done, or
another story about my dog, Purt). For
instance, a few weeks ago I was
transporting 5-year-old Vanessa (see my
column *Pray for Monkeys*) and two of her
boy cousins to the donut shop before
Sunday School. To reassure the cousins
that I was "safe", I asked Vanessa to tell
them how she and I had been friends for a
long time. She said: "Yes, you are my
bestest friend, and you will be my friend
until you die!".

That's true, but I wished she hadn't made it
sound as if I had a long, white beard (I had
a *short* white beard) and might pass on any
day now. Apparently, the kids at my church
aren't afraid to say just about <u>anything</u> to
"Mr. Kent" – last night, a little girl came up
to me and simply said: "Two." When I
asked if she was two years old, or if she
wanted two pieces of candy, she responded
by reciting her ABCs for me ("ABCDMSG...")
and then ran away. Kids operate on a

different system of logic than I (who operate on <u>no</u> system of logic at all).

My munchkins have also learned that they can usually get more than one piece of candy from Mr. Kent, simply by asking. Or, if I have extra, I'll just <u>tell</u> a kid that he/she can have two pieces, because "You're important!". And each little one certainly is important, special, and dear to my heart. Since the wife and I have no little ones (our youngest is 19), I'm happy to "Sugar them up and send them home!".

When I became involved in our wonderful church, I thought I might volunteer to work with the Senior crowd; driving them to/from events & outings, getting them backstage access at concerts (I know Bill Gaither's promoter)... but God instead <u>clearly</u> called me to work with the little ones. I had never worked with kids before, but I try to be obedient when He smacks me upside the head several times to get my attention.

The pitch was simple: volunteer to listen to kids recite their memory verses every Wednesday night. Well, I love the idea of anyone memorizing scripture, so I was happy to do what I could (though I <u>loved</u> Pastor Mark's Wednesday-night Bible studies). Since I never got to raise any little ones (I acquired my stepson, Ben, when he was 13), I thought this would be a chance to "fill in the blanks" by spending time with munchkins mumbling memory verses. But I was assigned to assist with the oldest group of kids, our pre-teens.

My job was still to assist the "real" teacher and listen to memory verses, but I also volunteered to bring the snacks (see my column *Planting Cupcakes*), so Ms. Sharon could concentrate on teaching. These kids weren't as cute as the Pre-K munchkins, but I did manage to make some friends among kids who would soon be "graduating" to our church's Youth ministry.

As these kids crossed into adolescence, I got to let them know that "Kent" (they don't have to call me "Mr." any longer) would still be their friend when they were teens – I promise to care about them even when they weren't "little kids". Because, increasingly, anyone under 25 seems like a kid to me. This reminds me of what an elder (age 90) once said about his nephew (age 75): "That Gus, he's a fine boy!".

This Fall, we'll graduate another group from the nurture of our <u>insane</u> Kid's Pastor

(Jeremy) to the care of our <u>giant</u> Youth Pastor (Lucas). I'll have more friends in the Youth group than before, and we'll get a new crop of Pre-K munchkins, who "Mr. Kent" has probably already met when they were toddlers. They're bound to say or do something else I'll find incomprehensible, or God will use them to teach me something new.

Don't worry – I'll share it with you. My wife says she's already heard about it waaaaay too much!

Speaking like this helps presenters hear themselves as the audience does

Brindle (my previous dog) knew when Daddy was sick

Love Letter to My Church

I'm not sure this letter is appropriate - is it proper to write a love letter to a <u>group</u>? I'm totally comfortable writing love letters to my wife (though she gets tired of reading about herself) - but if I wrote a letter to each person at my church who ministered grace to me when I showed up, alone, broken, lost, and afraid... there would be 100 letters, and (as one of my church folks says), "Ain't nobody got time for that!".

When I showed up that first Sunday morning, I fully intended to make my visit just the first of several I would make to area churches of the "Pentecostal/Charismatic" variety, so that I could assemble pluses/minuses with which to perform an unbiased comparison. That went out the window as soon as the Youth Pastor kicked off the worship time. It was intense, passionate, and it drew me in — I wanted to be part of that church. Then the Senior Pastor began his message, and I was immediately... amused.

It felt a little sacrilegious — growing up in a pastor's home, we didn't laugh about our father in his "Pastor" role — just in his "dad" role. But this man laughed at himself, and seemed to give us permission to laugh with him as he made up words, mispronounced Bible names and places, and (only half-seriously) threw in references to the Sooners. It was readily apparent that this Pastor wasn't "churchy"... but was just what I needed at that juncture.

Both of our full-time staff members (our Senior Pastor, Mark Fulks, and our Youth Minister, Chris Frye) refused to help me pity myself, and emphasized that, although they did not have all the answers to "fix" me, they knew Someone who could - and would - "build me back".

As I began to find my place as a functioning member of the church, I gravitated toward acts of service – I discovered long ago that there's always a place for people who don't mind doing the dirty work. My "dirty work" was to help clean tables toward the end of each of our fellowship dinners (we have a lot of meals together), and pass out water, tea, and coffee. I was soon made a formal member of the "Kitchen Crew", and received my own apron and secret decoder ring (OK, I'm still waiting on the decoder ring).

When I showed up to help cook and clean at a Valentines banquet, our Youth Pastor thought I had just showed up at church because I was lonesome (which I certainly was), and invited me to join the festivities as a guest. I already had a role, and we both got a laugh out of the misunderstanding, but I was touched by his concern and desire to include me.

And I can't count the times I came to the front for special prayer, but I do remember at least once when I mentioned to the man who most often prayed with me the general loneliness and specific sin that were my greatest obstacles. He has since graduated to a much livelier worship service – my friend, Mark Caldwell, now gets to worship the Lord in person. I also got to know some other "prayer warriors" that understood me - an amazing single lady who knew what my "traveling life" was like, and an older couple who have since "adopted" my wife and I.

My life is much different now, and I'm very involved in this community of believers, helping point hurting folks (like I was) to the Source of all healing. My goal is to become a helper like those who helped me so much. Now the church is helping my new family become a better picture of the refuge God wants us to be.

So, appropriate or not – I love y'all. Thank you, and I thank God for you!

Two of "my munchkins" from church – their Grandma brought them over to swim

Only Imagine

After a nephew of mine died short of his 2nd birthday, just a few years after I lost a friend in his early 20s to cancer, the losses started to mount up in my soul. As part of working through my struggle, I tried to imagine how Heaven must feel to them. Imagining how a child of less than 2 would interpret those experiences was really difficult, and I'm not confident that I did a good job of it, but my attempt was the genesis of a book that I'm still writing (see the excerpt in this book, 'Facets').

Imagining my young friend's experiences was a bit easier – I thought about how I might feel in awakening in an unfamiliar place and wondering if the experience was real (he died of bone cancer, and was on pretty heavy pain meds for months before he passed). As the story progressed in my mind, I added the imagined experiences of my saintly Grandmother (a tiny Hillbilly woman who could barely read and write), and a friend closer to my age who died in a car accident.

I threw in a few vignettes of how I imagined the Marriage Supper of the Lamb would go (there <u>will</u> be pizza!), and a worship concert featuring many different kinds of music (Bach to Punk to Bluegrass). Is my imagination accurate? Impossible – but not because I imagine too wildly, but because (as songwriter Keith Green put it): "God made the universe in 6 days, and He's been working on Heaven for 2,000 years!".

So the wildest I can <u>imagine</u> falls way short of the reality of what He designed for us. So, if Double-Pepperoni Pizza (thin crust, extra sauce) isn't there, He's got something even better waiting for me! If there aren't beautiful pine tree clearings for camping (including perfect 50-degree weather), there are experiences I'll enjoy even more. But none of those are what's gonna be really **cool** about Heaven.

The coolest thing, and what I can only imagine, is how I'll react when I see Jesus face to face. As the song ('I Can only Imagine') says, I wonder if I'll just collapse at His feet, hug his ankles, and cry, or grab His hands and twirl around with Him a few times (while I whoop!). And He'll be even happier to see me!

But, for a long time, I couldn't imagine that I'd really end up there. I'd been a believer for many years, when I had a dream one night that I was on an elevator with a few other folks. When I asked how far up we were going, one of them just responded: "All the way – Heaven!". Nothing else was said – I just leaned against the back wall and beamed contentedly.

No, I don't believe you have to have a meaningful dream to be confident of Heaven – but apparently, I needed it. And lots of folks I've known have already made the trip.

I recently lost some godly neighbors – the Abercrombies. For about a year, it was my privilege to visit with them, share cookies (he liked Snickerdoodles, she preferred Chocolate Chip), and pray. I was even called once to help lift Mr. Abercrombie off the bathroom floor. There's no truer message of acceptance than to be asked to help.

Though I've seen some photos of this couple from their younger days, I never got to know them at their physical peaks – only as their bodies finally wore out. I look forward to seeing them again when we'll all see so much more clearly. Of course, they're not the only folks with whom I look forward to reuniting.

Besides those I've already mentioned in this column, my Papa's been gone from this realm for more than 7 years. We didn't understand each other very well, though I'm probably more like him than any of my siblings – but we'll "know as we're known" there. Then there's my buddy Curtis, to whom I could have been a much better friend. And I look forward to hearing my step-grandfather Jess (who married my Mom's mom late in life) play the banjo again.

One of the most tender-hearted men I ever knew passed at about the age I am now, and I look forward to telling S.A. Tharp how much his kindness meant to me at a tough time in my adolescence. I look forward to hearing my Aunt Gracie talk to me again, without the raspy voice – in fact, hearing her voice <u>at all</u> will be doubly sweet, because she spent the last few years of her life with no voice (and she loved to talk!). And Ed Hurta taught me that a man didn't have to act like John Wayne (or my Dad) to be masculine.

So, while I love my life here (with my wife, who's much too good for me), "here" is not where I really belong. And, while I have lots of friends both old & young here, I have more every year "over there". Am I in a hurry? No. But, as Point of Grace sang, "*I'm not unhappy, but I'd leave today, if you'd let me, if you'd let me/ They may be clapping for me / But I'll wait / For you to come get me – come, come get me*".

Because I can only imagine...

To answer your deep theological question - Yes, there <u>will</u> be pizza in Heaven!

Just another reason to <u>love</u> living in East TX

Long as These Two Hands are Fit to Use

Merle Haggard penned a song many years ago called 'Working Man Blues', with the lyrics: *Hey, Hey, the workin' man, workin' man like me / I ain't never been on welfare, and that's one place I won't be / 'cause I'll be workin' / Long as these two hands are fit to use...* It's a catchy tune, and a blue-collar anthem.

I've been thinking about those lyrics lately, because I'm unemployed - again. After working for 8 years for an international consulting firm, helping organizations implement/upgrade an Oracle computer application (I'm a technical writer/trainer), I worked for a year for an outfit that just did training in the same application, and another year for a small consulting firm new to that application.

This particular computer application is going away, supplanted by a new one that performs the same functions better, faster, and/or cheaper, as the saying goes. In fact, the *new* software was created by the two guys who *invented* (back in the 1980s) the

76

application I've been teaching about for 12 years.

So, now I'm looking toward opportunities in new areas. For even longer than I've had "Trainer" in my job title, I've specialized in translating complex information (such as engineering or database jargon) into language easily understood by non-geeks) – yep, I'm a "Nerd Interpreter".

Having been unemployed three times within the last 2 years, I've learned some important lessons:

1. I'm more than just my paycheck or profession. My most important job is to know, love, and please God. Secondly, I'm a husband and a "Bonus Dad" to my wife's adult children. Third, I must take care of myself with rest, good food, recreation, etc. Work comes after those three priorities.

2. Plugging holes in the bucket is just as important as dipping more water. In other words, decreasing the amount of money we spend is just as beneficial as earning it. My biggest money-saving activity in the past three weeks has been to assemble enough tax deductions for 2018 to move us from

paying a few hundred dollars to getting a nice refund instead.

3. I'm much less patient with my own unsure future than when I have counseled friends in the same circumstances. Please understand, I have no excuse to be impatient with God about my next position – I can recount several times when He has provided just the right opportunity when I really needed it. I remember reading an ad once that seemed to be written expressly for me – and the job was even better when I got more information about it. One of my regular duties in that position was to host a group of tool salesmen at a Friday-night outing where we ate and played video games, or drove souped-up go-carts and mini-dragsters.

4. Naps are a gift from God – at 57, I love naps. After working for several hours on job applications, research, and writing samples, I'll occasionally give myself permission to join my lovely wife for an afternoon nap. It actually feels like a guilty pleasure.

5. <u>God</u> is my source – not any employer, and not the State of Texas (via Unemployment Insurance). That's much easier to preach to others than myself, but I've said it for years, and He has always come through.

Yes, we've burned through some savings, but we're making it just fine. Of course, I've been unemployed for all of a month – OK, God – it's time now, right?!?

6. Job scams are alive and well. During the past two weeks, I've heard from three different companies with "opportunities" to sell their insurance products or timeshare contracts, if I'm willing to pay for training, pay for leads, and lie to customers. Hmmm, let me think about that – No.

7. We live in a park. Waking up in my own bed morning after morning has reminded me of how amazing it is to live in East Texas, surrounded by greenery (even though some of it is parasitic and/or poisonous), near wonderful neighbors and our amazing church family. I've had the chance to "stop & smell the roses" (or honeysuckle). But I'm done now – right, God? Hello?

8. I am <u>not</u> in charge.

For offers of gainful employment (or to order a book, or to ask me how you, too, can snag an amazing wife), contact me at: sipeskent@gmail.com - *P.S. – By the grace of God, I am once again employed.*

Hello... I'm Mr. Ed

For those of you old enough to remember the 1960s TV sitcom "Mr. Ed", you'll remember that as the beginning of the show's introduction. I've been dying to answer my cell phone with that phrase, but there might be a prospective employer on the other end, screening me for a new position. The idea of beginning a job interview that way made me think of other really <u>dumb</u> things to do in an interview – here are a few more:

1. If asked the interview question: "Why do you think you're the <u>best</u> candidate for this job?" – try not to say:
- "I'm really <u>not</u>, but I'm the best you're gonna find for the **pathetic** amount you want to pay! No sweat, though - I'll make it up in stolen office supplies."

2. In response to the question: "What would you say is your greatest weakness?", don't say:
- "Well, my attendance is really poor, but my past employers said they didn't notice for a while, since I typically accomplished so little when I was there..."

3. In answer to the question: "What is your greatest strength?", you probably shouldn't say:
- "My talent for creative embezzlement – I've probably skimmed off over $200,000 in just the past 10 years!".

4. If an interviewer asks you to tell him "about a time when you had to think quickly to solve an emergency situation at work", you probably shouldn't bring up the time your manager caught you sleeping behind a pile of boxes in the stockroom.

5. When asked "Where do you see yourself in 5 years?", your answer probably shouldn't be:
- "I hope I'm not back in prison, homie!
- "Well, I hope I'm further along in my career than you are right now, lady – how old are you anyway, like 70?!?"

6. If the HR screener asks you to "Tell me about a time you had to work as part of a team to accomplish a challenging task.", don't tell the story of the time y'all drew straws to determine which employee would

punch the clock for the rest of the group while they went out for a "margarita lunch".

7. If asked about a time you took responsibility to make sure your work group succeeded, don't begin your story with:
- "One time our drug cartel knew we had a snitch, because our best mule was cavity-searched…"

8. If an interviewer asks you to name the last three books you read, don't ask:
- "You mean, like, books with, like <u>words</u> in them? OK – I remember one was 'Curious George and the Man in the Funny Hat'…"

9. When an interview begins with a request to "Tell me a bit about yourself – what makes you tick?", it's probably not an invitation for you to detail your recreational drug habit:
- "See, I start most weekdays – wait, today isn't Saturday, right? – Anyway, I start with an upper to get going, then I mellow out around 10 with a beer buzz, and by noon I'm usually asleep, wherever I'm sitting. Once I regain consciousness, the rest of my day is laser-focused on stealing to support the <u>serious</u> part of my habit… By the way, that's a <u>nice</u> watch!"

10. If the interviewer finishes her questions and offers to let you ask some, try to make them about the job or the company, not:

- "Hey, how 'bout them Cowboys!"
- "What's the least I can do and get away with it?"
- "Where's the best place in this building to hide from the cops?"
- "Would y'all mind if I brought my toddler into the factory with me? She don't take up much space – I can tape her feet together and set her in the corner!"
- "So, what's your favorite prison?"

My stepdaughter gave me a "Bonus Dad" t-shirt!

Cooking Guide for Men

When venturing into the unknown realm called the kitchen (for more than just heating a frozen pizza), men are required to adhere to the following principles:

1. There is no heat setting lower than "10" or "Maximum" on any stove or oven. All other settings are theoretical only. *Note: when baking, remember to open oven door at 30-second intervals to check doneness. Better yet, just leave the door open and use the broiler.

2. Measurements for spices are arbitrary – just open the top of whatever container holds the spice and dump some in. This will make your cooking much more interesting!

3. Only a few ingredients are needed for any (non-dessert) dish:
a) Meat
b) Potatoes
c) Onions
d) Garlic
e) Salt (Garlic salt qualifies)
f) Jalapeno (or more dangerous) pepper.

4. Dessert – don't bother, just buy some Blue Bell® and everyone will be happy. Remember that "Vanilla" is not a flavor. You can prove this to yourself by buying a carton of "Neapolitan" ice cream and noting the order in which the flavors are consumed: first Chocolate, then Strawberry, then Vanilla (possibly only to treat 2nd-degree burns (see #1).

5. Don't bother inviting women to try the results of your cooking – they won't understand why the outside is charred and the inside raw. She will probably also comment that its' flavor is "interesting", "intense", and/or "toxic". This also might be a good time to mention that you should keep the phone number for the Poison Control Center handy.

6. Expiration dates – like cooking heat levels below maximum, these are imaginary. To prove this, simply buy a carton of yogurt and don't open it until at least a month after its "expiration date" – it'll still be disgusting.

7. Every dish is better with bacon. Try this classic sandwich – the BLBTB – bacon, lettuce, bacon, tomato, bacon. If you don't

have tomatoes or lettuce in your fridge, just leave them out – they're not really food items, merely decorations. Short on bread? Just wrap the ingredients in bacon!

8. Outdoor cooking – the bigger the fire, the faster you can get back to more important outdoor activities, such as hiking to the ER. Note that burning tires will produce a very hot flame, and, as an added benefit, will add a unique flavor to whatever you cook over them.

9. You can also cook food wrapped in heavy-duty aluminum foil using campfire coals (you might want to let the flames die down a bit before trying this). Simply place all ingredients in a foil pouch, bury in the coals, and pull the foil out a few hours (or days) later. Better yet, just leave the pouch where it is, thus decreasing the chances its contents will harm people or animals.

10. When planning how much food you will need for a given number of guests, use this handy algorithm: Multiply the number of people you're expecting by the square root of Pi, add your age in dog years, then divide by the number of sheets left on the toilet paper roll in your bathroom. Then

ignore the resulting number and just fill up a shopping cart – when it's full, you will have enough ingredients. If it turns out you don't have enough, simply send away the excess guests on a fake errand, such as "fetching lettuce", then flee the country.

My fellow deacon, Lin, who really _does_ know how to cook!

Money Talks... but Not Very Loudly

As an American, I hold the firm belief that money can accomplish anything – if the Waffle House menu doesn't show a 3-egg breakfast, I just tell the server what I want, and he/she charges me the correct amount. When I need work done around our property, I tell one of my skilled friends what we need done, he tells me about what it will cost, and we get it done.

But a few years ago, I went on the hunt for my favorite hard candy – Peach Jolly Ranchers. The Peach Kisses were no longer available individually, nor were the candy sticks. The only way to get Peach was in a "Passion Fruit" mix, and each bag contained only 6-7 Peach Kisses. So I called the factory and asked the price for 500 Peach Kisses – and the "customer service" person simply told me they did not sell Peach kisses apart from the aforementioned assortment.

As I told Customer Service – "Y'all <u>make</u> the candy there – just put a bag at the end of the Peach Kiss assembly line, stop at 5 pounds, and quote me a price!". I knew they didn't *package* them for retail sale like that, since I'd searched for years and contacted multiple candy distributors. I'd even tried other Peach hard candy (from the ATL airport), but nothing matched the Jolly Ranchers. But I went directly to the source, and was still rebuffed.

This baffled me – I thought that, if I was willing to pay for a legal product, I could buy whatever I wanted. But here was a manufacturer refusing to sell me what I wanted, at any price! But this is America – I should be able to purchase what I want, shouldn't I?

I've even checked candy distributors on the Internet – though I enter "Peach Jolly Rancher" and "bulk", all I get are links to companies selling every other flavor. I'm hoping I don't have to buy 50 bags of 'Passion Fruit Mix' to get 300 or so Peach Kisses.

Maybe I'll try bribery – surely someone at the factory can be persuaded to bag up 300 Peach Kisses for me, "under the table". I can see myself meeting my "connection" in a dimly-lit alley somewhere. I'll display the cash, my connection will display the merchandise (I'll require a taste sample), and we'll make the exchange.

Now, I know what you're thinking: "How can you be sure of purity? After all, you're dealing with a criminal!". But I need my Peach JR fix, and I'm willing to take that risk - I have priorities. Hmm... maybe I should be "packing", in case the deal goes bad – but will my BB rifle provide sufficient firepower?

I buy lots of candy, especially when I'm going through an airport or to church, so I suppose I could just buy the 'Passion Fruit' assortment, and give "my kids" the Strawberry, Raspberry, and Watermelon Kisses, but there's a moral principle involved here. And no, "my kids" probably wouldn't be invited to share my "Peach" Kisses – hey, I love them, but there's a limit!

OK, I might give a few of them the opportunity for a taste of "Fruity Nirvana", but only the ones who I believe can truly appreciate the gift. Maybe I'll hold a contest, in which the 3 kids who guess a number, between 1 and 17 billion, closest to the one I've determined ahead of time (which is always "7"), get a Peach Kiss.

And maybe I'll start a national campaign to "Bring Back Peach!". Why, if all my loyal readers would join me in signing a petition to the Jolly Rancher company, that'd be... four of us. OK, so, returning to my "back alley" plan...

Yep, We are Country!

We have a "country" home – it's not that we just live outside a small town, but that so many of our structures are "rigged". A more polite way to express the ways in which things on our property have been made to work is "Southern-engineered". When we bought the property, it had been mostly abandoned for 7 years, and there was a lot to fix, clean up, and burn (see my articles *Blood, Sweat, and...*, *Burnin' Down the House*).

This started with the deck around our above-ground pool. The pool was a genuine herpetarium – a snake pit. It was also home to frogs, and other unidentified undesirables. The liner was cracked and torn, so we had it replaced. However, to do so, the installers had to remove about 1' of our deck on 3 sides – we said "Sure!". The deck was in bad shape anyway – with huge splinters, warped boards, and a color that matched the house – faded, vague brownish tan.

After the new liner was in, we wondered how to deal with the 6" gap this left between the edge of the pool railing and the deck boards. The answer? Don't bother! The gaps have existed for over 4 years, and we just warn people to watch out for them. I'm amazed I haven't yet stepped into the gap and tested my ability to do the splits (or hit really high vocal notes!).

We did repaint the deck, using a heavy-duty paint containing sand (for traction). But we didn't bother to prep the deck surface, so we now have huge swaths of rust-colored paint peeling from it. The dark red surface has another advantage: on an August afternoon, I can cook hot dogs on it! Or I can produce 2nd-degree burns on the bottoms of my feet, while I dance an entertaining jig, whine, and say colorful words (like "Darn!).

Toward the beginning of August, the water in our pool usually becomes too warm to be "refreshing" – in fact, with more jets, it could qualify as a hot tub. My plan to mitigate this has been to get a plumber friend of ours to run another water line into the shallow end of the pool (both the skimmer and water inlet are on the deep end), ending in a fountain. We're thinking the water mist would be cooled by the air, making that end of the pool a bit nicer. But I got up from my nap last Sunday to find that my wife had turned on the lawn sprinkler, which was hitting the pool at one end of its arc – problem solved!!

I have two gates on my property which lead to our back acre, both of which currently swing on heavy-duty zip ties. The door to our chicken run is attached to its frame with duct tape, because the bottom part of the door rotted away, taking the hinge with it. The decorative posts in front of the chicken house overhang (it used to be a pool house) display an inch of space between their bottoms and the top of the porch.

My garage has two rows of brand-new wood siding on one bottom wall, an improvement on the gaping hole it showed for the past month (I removed some rotten boards, one of which had a mushroom growing from it), except that the bottom row of siding is shorter than the others, making it necessary to make a horizontal cut – apparently, something of which I'm incapable. I already ruined one piece of siding by first trying to trim it to the correct height, then attempting to <u>force</u> it into place with repeated hammer blows. After I got a second piece trimmed to length, and *thought* I'd trimmed its height correctly as well... I just left it, half in place, half out.

Granted, none of these quick fixes are unique to the country – if I lived in a suburban home, I'd probably still have some part of it held together with duct tape. Part of the reason so <u>many</u> things on my country property are "sort of" fixed is that we have things we probably wouldn't have in the suburbs – like my 30x40' shop, its doors held closed with cinder blocks.

If I soon become employed again, I'll be ready to hire someone with actual skills to <u>really</u> fix more of what's broken on our property. Of course, we'll still have to prioritize the jobs to be done – my handyman doesn't have the time to fix everything, and his wife wants him to fix some of the broken things around their house, too. The other option is for me to learn <u>actual</u> homeowner skills... and I'm not sure we can afford the emergency room visits that would require.

In the meantime, I should probably get some more zip ties...

Your Call is Very Important to Us

Recently, I spent several hours on hold in "Telephone Hell", and I'm convinced that there's customized eternal punishment reserved for the folks who design these systems. One insurance billing service <u>repeatedly</u> disconnected my call after I'd been on hold for at least 20 minutes. Below are a few observations I made during that experience:

"*Your call is very important to us*"... "But not so much that we have staffed more than 2 employees to answer the 12,000 calls we receive each day."

"*All of our agents are currently assisting other callers...*" "Your call will be ignored in the order it was received."

"*Your current wait time is longer than 2 minutes*"... "by about 3 hours, in fact!".

"*You can avoid waiting on hold, by using our website*"... "...which contains a wealth of general information about our processes, but not the single piece of data crucial to your success!".

"*Rather than continuing to hold, press 1 to request a callback...*" "which will never happen. It's wishful thinking on both your part and ours, especially if both of our customer service agents go off-shift within the next hour. Expect us to call back on the 12th of Never, you gullible fool!".

Our pastor recently preached a series entitled 'One Minute After you Die', and one of the messages was on Hell. Here's how I imagine the experience of a Call Center manager in the afterlife: He waits in line for 90 days to use a single phone labeled "Relief Hotline". After being on hold for 11 hours, listening to Celine Dion played over a horrific, scratchy speaker, his call is disconnected, seemingly at random. He then moves to the back of the line, to endlessly repeat the process.

I once almost took a job training telemarketers, but the slave galley called with a better offer (if you don't understand this reference, check out the classic movie 'Spartacus'). Seriously, that would have been "going to the Dark Side" for me – one of the reasons we disconnected our landline telephone was because telemarketers seemed to be the only ones calling it.

One of the folks I met on a flight for work owned a company that mined the audio files of client customer hotlines, analyzing trends for actionable data. In English, that means they looked for repeated words, then recommended to the client what really interested (or bothered) their customers. Since I love "making mischief", I plan to call a few of these customer hotlines to mess with their data.

Here's how I imagine that call would go:

"Hello, this is American Delta United airlines – your only choice for air travel since 2022, and I'm incessantly perky! How may we not help you today?"

My response: "Burple is the noise you make after drinking grape juice too quickly."

"Sorry, I didn't quite get that – please repeat it."

Me: "Lycanthropy!"

"Please choose from the following options – to hear your options in English, press or say 1..."

Me: "Inclement. Propitiation. Camera oscura!"

"I still didn't get that – please repeat it once more."

Me: "Does your chewing gum lose its' flavor on the bedpost overnight?"

"I'm still not understanding you. Let me get someone on the line who can help you!"

...at which point a real, live customer service person (the poor fool!) is forced to speak with me.

...and I begin to attempt conversation using mumbled names of Italian dishes to pretend that I speak that language ("Eggplant parmesan?" "Linguini Bolognese!" "Fettucine! Mangia fettucine!!")

...and then the poor customer service agent surrenders and disconnects the call, and I'm left with a beatific smile on my face. As the old Klingon (from *Star Trek*, of course) proverb goes: "Revenge is a dish best served cold."

Hiking to Hell

I'm in the San Francisco area for 2 days, for a job interview. I have the chance to use a different software than the one I've taught for 12 years. That particular suite of applications is going away, replaced by this one – but... that's not why you called.

After two video interviews and a presentation to two "live" folks and two by video, then a final "live" interview with the head honcho, I was worn out. My hotel was pretty close, "as the crow flies", but I don't happen to fly. As both of my loyal readers might remember (Hi, Mama!; Hello, Dona!), I've been fighting a couple of bulging discs that at one point made it terribly painful to walk for more than a few steps. After months of treatment, exercises, and hanging upside down, I'm walking much better. So... I punched up on my phone directions to the hotel.

Unfortunately, there's quite a bit of construction going on in the office complex where my interviews were held, so there's no way to walk <u>directly</u> to any destination. I asked a security guard how to reach my hotel, and he gave me some general guidance ("So, you go through this office complex, and when you get back out to the street, take a right. Your hotel is less than 100 yards away.") This man was a liar, and probably an agent of Satan... OK, maybe he was just bad at giving directions...

I got through the office complex and turned right. All I could see were buildings carrying the logo of the company I'm trying to join, plus a few others – but no hotels were in sight. I stopped two construction workers, but they had no idea where the Marriott was. Another guy walking while looking at his laptop told me he didn't know, but offered to pull up directions for me (folks in SF are so polite!).

After walking for what seemed like 2 miles (in dress shoes), I finally saw, very high but seemingly close, the beautiful Marriott sign. At that point, the sign might as well have said "Cold water, restroom, air conditioning, bed flop!", because I suddenly had renewed hope. I began to walk briskly in the direction of my last sighting of "the sign", because it once again disappeared behind more four-story office buildings. I finally spotted a mall, and recalled that my hotel was, indeed, near a mall.

I made a right, and spotted a Marriot vehicle in a parking lot – I thought that must be the parking lot for my hotel. After illegally crossing two busy lanes of traffic (maybe my wife won't read this...), my actual hotel was in sight!

But which way to turn – should I trudge through the parking lot (at the back of the hotel) and go all the way around the building to find the front entrance, or try walking along the fence, beside the exit ramp for the expressway? Of course, I picked the wrong direction (see my column *I've Been Lost here Before!*), and began to trudge along the busy roadway, then turned to walk the wrong way along an exit ramp. I thought there <u>must</u> be a front entrance somewhere along there!!

There was only a 5-foot chain-link fence, surrounded by a border of trees, greenery, and an increasingly-deep ditch between the trees and ground cover. 15 years ago, I would have sneered at such a barrier, thrown my laptop bag over, then clambered over it myself. But not now; not at 57. If I had attempted the climb, someone would have found me, possibly days later, lying on my face in the ditch and shouting at raccoons not to steal my bag.

102

I walked all the way to the front of the hotel, and past it, thinking I would see an entrance open to drivers (and pedestrians). I could see the Marriott sign, right in front of my face, level with the highway where I was walking. But there was a steep, grassy slope and the chain-link fence... 20 feet below.

My goal was so close!! I couldn't help but think of the story Jesus told of the rich man and the beggar - the rich man, in Hell, looked up at formerly "poor Lazarus", now in the Old Testament version of Heaven - happy, in great health, and hanging out with the Hebrew patriarch, Abraham. A big part of the rich guy's torment came from being able to <u>see</u> how well the former beggar was doing and comparing their respective conditions. But "a great gulf" was between the two vastly different locations.

I turned around and trudged the half mile back to the parking lot entrance, made my way past the pool exits, employee entrance, and picnic tables, to the beautiful front entry. The cool, filtered air felt wonderful, as did the citrus-infused water. I drank two cups immediately, but decided to "let go of some other water" before drinking more. Finally, I made it to my room and reached "the Promised Land", where, after a visit to the "coffee recycling station", I collapsed on the beautiful mattress.

This proves to me once again that I should <u>never</u> leave my hotel unless accompanied by a responsible adult. I'm not very brave when I travel, anyway. My first week working in Manhattan (*New York, New York!*), I became confident enough to find the correct subway entrance, avoid looking rats in the eye, and travel to my client offices, 20 blocks away (in Madison Square Garden). But in my 2nd week, I made a friend with another newbie Consultant and walked to a restaurant 6 blocks from our hotel – I knew his sense of direction <u>had</u> to be better than mine.

By the end of my 6-week assignment, my buddy, Josh, and I had made treks to Coney Island, Queens, Long Island, Harlem, and one interesting area that resembled my mental picture of a Maine fishing town. Yes, I'm willing to explore, provided someone else is being brave *for* me... or at least sharing the misery of being lost in a strange city. Apparently, for me, it's all about having <u>someone</u> <u>else</u> to blame.

Joce says I look like a little homeless man when I don't shave for a week

I'm Shellfish

There's an old joke about an oyster who refused to share his pearl – he was... yeah, you guessed it – shellfish. Now, as I've grown up, I've learned to be more generous, but for a long time, I wasn't willing to give anything that would require me to do without. And if giving doesn't require me to do without, it's not a sacrifice. It's still a <u>good</u> thing to do, but it might not be the **best**.

We have a family goal – I want to earn enough to comfortably send 3 kids to our church's Kid's Camp, and 3 to our Youth Camp, every summer. Now, we're not doing that yet (though we've sent 1-2 in previous years). And, before anyone thinks I'm patting myself on the back, I'm <u>actually</u> being selfish – I want to have a part in sending our kids off to camp because our church camp (Mountain View, near Jacksonville, TX) helped deepen my spiritual life as an adolescent, and I badly want that for the kids & youth of my church.

I'm 57 at this writing (and beginning to feel it!), and I'm very conscious of where my time, energy, and dollars are going. Having a part of making the next generation godly men & women is a very big deal to me! It's such a big deal that, when my sweet wife told me I should consider replacing the Dodge Ram (180K miles) I've been driving with a nice, new F150 (I'm a Ford guy), I decided I'd rather put the $$ elsewhere.

But, I promise you, it's not because I'm a super-nice guy. I'm just a guy who loves "my munchkins", and I'm more interested in seeing them grow into a deep love life with the Lord than I am in getting a "sweet ride". But I am a **guy**.

So every year or so, I'll go on the Ford Truck website and "build a vehicle". I start with the XLT package and add from there. I hate small cabs, so I select the Extra Cab, and the 8' bed is a good thing to have. Cloth seats wear out and show dirt quickly, so leather is my choice. And heated seats feel nice on my low back.

The F-150 isn't available in purple, and Ford almost never offers "Grabber Blue" on anything but the Mustang, but they offer a nice teal this year. I stink at backing with a trailer, and there's a "Backup Assist" offered this year that would help me. Backup cameras are standard on all new vehicles, and I need that help, too. And there's an option of built-in loading ramps, plus a spray-in factory bedliner.

I'm still not pleased with factory sound systems (though they're better than they used to be), so I'll still need to add an aftermarket subwoofer and more powerful door/dash speakers, plus an amp to drive them, and a 10-band EQ. After all, what good's a cushy, cool vehicle if it's not also a rolling Rock/Rap arena? (My poor wife just doesn't understand.)

A few years ago, I got to drive around a Grabber Blue Mustang while on an assignment in San Diego, CA. The suspension felt like driving a brick, but I did feel cool tooling around in it, and I loved the feeling of pulling into Sonic for dinner! The only thing that could have made the situation any better would have been a convertible top, but I was not complaining.

The long and short of all this is that I have vehicle fantasies, like most guys (and my wife loves her Cadillac SUV). But the vehicle I drive is more a tool than a support for my ego, or an expression of my personality. As long as the Ram keeps running, I'll probably continue to drive it, because it's more important to me to invest my money in kids & youth, through my wonderful church! Sure, it's selfish, but in the long run, people usually act in their own self-interest – and I am interested in the next generation!

Kent in his current truck – <u>not</u> an F-150

Coffee, Coffee, Coffee!!!

I'm a coffee snob. I know that the term for someone who knows a lot about wine is an Oenophile, but I'm not sure the term for a coffee lover – but I am. I clearly remember being bemused by my best friend's parents' love for coffee when we were in college – they always had a pot brewing, and my friend's younger brother even worked at a fancy coffee store in our local mall, years before anyone in Texas had heard of Starbucks. At the time, I only knew of two kinds of coffee: really horrible and OK.

Really horrible coffee was the dregs of a pot that had been sitting on a burner at Jack in the Box since noon, when I'd buy a cup just to get warm while waiting for Mama to pick me up from high school. I'd grimace at each sip – no amount of cream or sugar was sufficient to overcome its bitterness. When I became an adult, I joined the ranks of coffee drinkers, but I never there was anything better than Folgers® or Maxwell House® out there.

I began the coffee habit early, as an 8-year-old in our many church socials. As a preacher's kid, I was at all of them, and coffee was usually all there was to drink besides water. I took mine with lots of cream and sugar – more of a dessert than a drink, really. As an adult, working as a supervisor in a cable plant on a 12- to 18-hour shift, I would drink at least 4 pots of pretty bad coffee each night, just to remain conscious and break the monotony. And I purposely bought some really bad, cheap coffee as a joke once, to send to my Uncle Bob, who had often griped about "truck stop" coffee. I bought him a brick of coffee in a plain, white label, thinking he would get the joke.

Like much of my humor, it was not perceived by him as a joke, and he brewed a pot, drank it, then remarked later about how *horrible* it was. That reminded me of some more "lost humor" – during my first trip to NYC as a consultant, I sent some souvenirs back to my co-workers at Mizzou, where I'd worked a few months earlier. One of the more interesting characters in the Cashiers department was a guy named Stan, an ex-Navy Petty Officer whose job was to cancel students who didn't pay their tuition in time.

Just after the start of each semester, Stan would hold up his right index finger, smile, and announce that his "cancel finger" was ready. He acted as if he enjoyed the experience, and he even got a nickname around the office: The Dream Crusher. So, as a joke, I bought him a cheap NYC souvenir coffee mug, covered it carefully in bubble wrap, then smashed it.

I then put all the tiny shards in a plastic bag and placed the bag carefully into a box labeled "For the Dream Crusher". I thought Stan would get the joke, but, no, he assumed the mug had spontaneously exploded into tiny shards during shipping – he thought he'd been cheated out of his NYC souvenir. (By the way, Stan just acted as if he enjoyed cancelling students – I often witnessed him working very hard to help a student build a payment plan that would allow him/her to stay in school – he just acted mean.)

As part of my Masters (Journalism) studies, I was required to put together a Strategic Communication plan for an organization. This organization could be real or fictitious, but I had recently read of a non-profit group that was selling Rwandan coffee, and using the revenue to make micro-loans to Rwandan war widows (from the genocide that had occurred there) with which they established their own small businesses. I liked what they were doing, so I purchased a bag of their coffee – and I was amazed!

I contacted someone from the non-profit group the next day, and he immediately accepted my proposal to create a communication plan for Land of a Thousand Hills (LOTH) coffee. He also offered to send me free bags of coffee for as long as I was working on their communication plan. I accepted, and decided to try a bag of their Dark Roast – oh, my! Imagine rich hot chocolate, but without sugar. This is the only coffee I can enjoy without cream or sugar – it's <u>that</u> good.

It turns out that Rwanda is one of the world's premier coffee-growing regions (coffee was first consumed as a beverage in Ethiopia), but most coffee from there was sold as "commodity coffee" (the cheapest, generic kind), because the growers didn't know how to properly grow, harvest, sort, and clean gourmet coffee beans. The LOTH project (in partnership with the US Agriculture department) trained Rwandans for two years, established processing stations in several regions of the country, and began selling the coffee via an e-commerce website.

Since LOTH was based near Atlanta, GA, I even got to visit its headquarters one day while working in the area. Their coffee house there smells sooooo good! I even purchased bags of LOTH coffee for everyone in my family for Christmas one year, because I loved it so much – they were a bit confused about why I was giving them groceries.

Since that time, I've discovered other coffees that I love nearly as much as Rwandan – Sumatra is very good, Ethiopian Yirgacheffe is excellent, and Columbian is pretty good. There are also some I don't like that much, even though they're popular – Kona from Hawaii is just too mild, and I don't care for any kind of coffee that's "French-roasted" – it tastes burned.

So, yeah – I'm a coffee snob. But don't worry, if I come to your house, and you offer me Folgers®, Maxwell House®, or something else that's not "gourmet", I'm not going to snub it. But, if you're a friend of mine, you might get a bag of coffee that I <u>really</u> like as a gift. Just nod & smile – pretend you understand.

*Working the Health Fair with one of the best
men I know – my "little bro", Barry*

Musical Theology 201

Many of our classic hymns come from a time in which Christian Education was geared toward the masses who couldn't read – they taught, in music, what we would teach today in print (or via webinar). Now, even though I'm an avid reader, I've also gotten some pretty cool revelations from listening to Christian music, even from songwriters many folks might consider not to be very deep. One of those is Peter Furler, former frontman (and major songwriter) for the Newsboys.

He started a new band with an old buddy from the Newsboys (Phil Joel, also a pretty deep songwriter), and wrote a song called *Lazarus*. Now, I had always sort of bought the idea that the shortest verse in the Bible (Jesus wept) showed us Jesus' humanity in being sad that His friend had suffered and died without his buddy Jesus being there (or something like that). But the concept never sat well with me – why mourn over

116

something Jesus knew He was going to fix in the next 5 minutes?

This song presents a different take on that scripture, which opens up a whole new line of thought: Jesus wept because He knew what this future-dated check He was writing (in resurrecting & healing his friend Lazarus) would cost Him. Isaiah 53 says "...by His wounds we were healed", which tells me that all healing (even the "natural" healing our cells perform) was bought by Jesus, for all time, on the cross.

He also wept because He knew the Pharisees would still not trust Him as the Messiah, even after they'd seen someone they knew to be dead rise and hop out of his tomb. In fact, the Pharisees decided they'd have to have Lazarus killed along with Jesus in order to retain their power and position. That reminds me of the story Jesus told of another Lazarus, a beggar, and a "rich man".

They both died, and were immediately in very different circumstances – the beggar was comforted and content for eternity to come, while the rich guy was in torment. He asked Abraham to send Lazarus to his brothers, to keep them from ending up like himself, because, of course, "They'll believe someone risen from the dead!". Uh, no. Still not gonna happen – they'll find some excuse to **still** refuse to change.

Part of the lyric that always gives me chills says: "*It's alright, you can open your eyes now/ And through the shroud, hear my voice, over the crowd / This is not for you, but if you knew, what it would signify / You would know just why I cry / I cry...*"

It's amazing to me that the Pharisees weren't <u>afraid</u> of Jesus – if He could bring someone back from the dead, couldn't He <u>make</u> someone else dead just by **commanding** it? They also saw Him reattach an ear that one of his disciples cut off with a sword – didn't <u>any</u> of them think, "Um... hold on a minute. I've never seen that done before... If this guy can put an ear <u>back where it belongs</u> on the side of a guy's head, what's to say He couldn't stick a <u>third</u> one right in the middle of my forehead, or replace my ears with additional **nostrils**?!?".

But maybe they'd heard the messages about The Father's mercy and grace (two distinct ideas) that Jesus so often taught, and they figured He'd avoid negative

118

actions like "smoting them" (as my Pastor says). And they were right... for now. But, as an old Christian Rock song (from DeGarmo & Key) says, ...*Last time He came, to save the lost / Crowned Him with thorns, put Him on a cross / When He comes back, be no place to hide / You best be sure that you are on His side!*

The point of this article? When the Bible tells us to "fear God and live", there's a reason. He's got all power, and it's just His Mercy that keeps Him from making grease spots of us all, because we do disappoint Him, it is a big deal, and Somebody had to pay.

Theology 201 – He did. But it's a limited-time offer!

Wearing the Dad Shoes

My nephew Toby has a quirky sense of humor, and a decidedly throwback sense of style. A couple of years ago, he bought his first house, a 1970s era 2-story (think "Brady Bunch"), complete with avocado-colored kitchen, yellow wallpaper, and other "period" features. He also purchased a 1970s-era Cadillac convertible, just for tooling around town. At his birthday party last year, he noted my white New Balance shoes and asked me why I wasn't manning the grill.

Of course, I looked at him oddly, though I'm sort of used to his quirky comments. He explained to me that white NB shoes are an "Internet Meme", associated with manning the grill at family events, delivering life lessons, and performing other "Dad" activities. And here I thought my shoes were still "cool"!

I was a bit disturbed by his characterization of me, based on just my shoes, until I gave it a bit more thought, and I now wear the "Dad shoes" with pride. I've written a couple of articles ('Being the Dad', 'I *Was* the Dad') about how much I love the role of Dad in my new family – I get to help parent a 19-year-old in college, and I'm the "Bonus Dad" (Hi, Jess!!) to our married 20-something daughter. Their birth Dad, Brian, lost a bout with cancer 16 years ago.

Verily, I am "<u>The</u> <u>Dad</u>" (cue trumpet fanfare). If there's a dirty job to be done (burying a dead chicken, killing a snake, crawling under the house - which I hope I <u>never</u> have to do again), or cleaning up dog vomit... it's mine. Yes, as a single mom for several years, my wife has certainly proven that she's <u>capable</u> of performing these actions, but if I'm at home, those are "Dad duties". I also lift heavy things, eliminate stumps, take our vehicles in for servicing, and reset the router when necessary.

Unfortunately, there are a lot of tasks around our place for which I'm not equipped, such as anything requiring boards to be sawn, pipes to be replaced, or A/C units to be... whatever that equipment periodically requires – possibly, the incantation of magic spells. For those jobs, I must hire a "Real Man". Now, my wife is likely to chide me for saying this (because she loves me), but I'll admit that guys with those sorts of skills intimidate me – all I can do is pay them whatever they say is fair, and occasionally hand them something.

I do have <u>other</u> skills – if one of those Real Man types needs a resume, I can create if for him. If his computer has a virus, he might call me to get rid of it (I have <u>the best</u> virus checker). And if he needs to learn how to give a speech, I'm the guy. If he's hungry, I can whip up some beautiful BBQ chicken. Because, fortunately, being a "Real Man" is about more than carpentry skills, plumbing savvy, or A/C wizardry.

It's about keeping commitments, working hard (at whatever I <u>can</u> do), and leading by example. It's about being kind to children and older folks, and helpful to those in between. It's about giving, and protecting others. And more than anything, being an "RM" means humbling myself before God, acknowledging Him as the true Source for my family, the giver of all good gifts. As I tell my munchkins whenever I get the chance, everything good comes from God – I just get to pass along some of it!

"Dad duty" – it's not always pretty, and it's certainly not always what I feel like doing. I'm usually the last one awake (making sure the dogs & chickens are set for the night, the house is locked up, and the coffee's ready to brew the next morning) and the first one up (making breakfast). And I'm learning to do some things for myself, like fixing minor problems with my riding mower (I can replace my own blades now – hope I get to keep my fingers!).

Unfortunately, I still get overwhelmed by some projects, such as replacing the rotten boards on the side of my garage ("So, mushrooms growing from the wall is a <u>bad</u> thing?!?"). I removed (and burned up) the rotten wood, then bought what I thought were suitable replacement boards. They don't seem to fit the same as the old ones, so I now have a hole in my garage wall. Good thing my wife is an understanding woman!

And I have some Real Man phone numbers programmed into my phone – just in case.

...In All the Wrong Places

My first foray into "computer dating" came after my 50th birthday. When I first got married, in 1992, personal computers were certainly around (though not common), but the Internet was just a few computer nerds exchanging messages. So, when I involuntarily became single again, I tried a couple of dating sites (such as Christian Mingle), just to see what my chances were.

It turns out that my chances for a new romance were excellent, and that many cute, 20-year-old girls wanted to meet me! Then I realize that they were looking at the income I reported, rather than my photos or bio. Surprisingly (Ha!), as soon as I removed my answer to the "income" question, I got no more "hits" from cute, young girls. Nor did I get hits from beautiful 30-year-old women.

So I narrowed my goal and my search pattern, and I established strict requirements for women with whom I'd correspond:

1. They had to be breathing.
2. They had to be <u>actual</u> females.

No, really, I wrote a letter to God, asking Him for specific things in the lady with whom I planned to spend the rest of my life, such as:

1. Passionately in love with Him
2. Kind (as opposed to "nice")
3. Not as fat as me (Yes, ladies, I know that's hypocritical, but thanks for your input!)
4. Affectionate (no gutter thoughts here)
5. Liked me.

That last qualification might seem like a no-brainer, but I had spent more than 20 years with a woman who pretty much disliked me (granted, I wasn't as likeable back then), and often told me about it. The goal of finding a lady who would really like me seemed like a real stretch.

I corresponded with a few ladies, but it seemed as if everyone my age was interested mostly in "knitting". There were a few exceptions – one lady advertised that she loved "muddin!". I just wanted someone who'd play racquetball with me, and maybe keep up when we went mountain biking.

Most ladies are, understandably, cautious when meeting someone with whom they've only corresponded via e-mail, text, or phone, but one lady actually sent me a message that stated, "I'm drunk – you should come over!". Ah... No. Emphatically – "NO!" (insert mental picture of me, running away scared, as fast as I could).

That particular contact was severed, almost immediately. I corresponded with a few other ladies, mostly divorced, but at least one who was widowed. She seemed like an excellent mom, and a real believer – but I didn't think I was ready to help raise 3 teenage girls (insert mental picture of me ripping out tufts of my hair, like Larry in The Three Stooges).

I had a few "in-person" dates before I met the lovely Jocelyn. One lady, a 40-something elementary school teacher, told me that she wanted a relationship with someone who would attend Southern Gospel concerts with her. Ah...No. Neither could I see her head-banging with me at a Skillet show. Nothing against Southern Gospel, I just had too much of it as a kid – I learned what to expect from the performance of every singing group that visited our church – at some point, most songs would end with the tenor going really high, and the bass singer really low, everything backed by steel guitar.

All in all, I <u>hated</u> dating. When Jocelyn and I became "an item", I informed her that "dating" was not my goal – I was "courting" her. Dates are fun, but I had already figured out that I don't do well as a solo act – I need to be half of a duet. Or maybe it's a trio, because my wife and I are both "involved" in a relationship with the Lord that's even more important than our relationship with each other. And neither Jocelyn nor I sing "lead" in this show – **He** does.

I Have a Pony...

*Note – Purt is no longer an adolescent –
and it's my firm hope that he's stopped
growing!*

Steven Wright, one of my favorite
comedians, says, "My building allows pets...
I have a pony." Coming home from my
traveling job, I'm greeted by my adolescent
dog, Purt, who increasingly resembles a
pony – maybe a Shetland colt. My wife and
I are thinking of having a custom saddle
made, so he can give rides to the neighbor
kids. Maybe we can even charge them for
it, and use that revenue to defray the huge
amount we're spending on dog food.

In my first article about my new puppy, I
attached the photo below, in which he was
dwarfed by a sheet of paper. His head is
now bigger than his entire body was in that
first photo. And I don't think he realizes
how large he is – he seems mystified that
he can no longer fit beside me in an
armchair, or wriggle through the fence
around the pool (or, as he thinks of it,
"Purt's giant water bowl").

Purt is definitely "the big dog" around our house now, though he still knows who's "top dog" (that's me, unless my wife says otherwise). He knows when "Dad" isn't home, too – he mopes, either in an armchair in our bedroom or on the couch. But this moping looks remarkably like the napping he does most of the time when I'm there.

We recently bought a microfiber L-shaped couch, with a lounge, and Purty loves to nap on it – he takes up a whole section. But since it's microfiber, he occasionally slides off onto the wood floor, where his 75# bulk makes a solid "Clunk!". Purt always looks up confusedly, as if to say, "How'd I get down here?".

When I sit on our couch now, I'm at eye-level with Purt as he's standing, and he thinks this is a perfect time to examine (with his 6" tongue) my whole face for remains of anything interesting I might have smeared on there during the past several hours. He does a thorough search every time, just in case. I try to keep my lips closed, then I go wash my face again.

He "officially" lives outside – he sleeps on the back corner porch, and he's attached to a cable around a huge oak tree when we're gone. But if we're home and awake, he's with us, inside or out. I keep losing outdoor shoes – he'll chew both of them, and leave one from any pair in our yard. I now own several lone shoes, slippers, and flip-flops of various unmatched types. If there's ever an emergency that requires us to evacuate the house, I'll be the guy wearing a New Balance cross-trainer on one foot and a soggy house slipper on the other.

Purt hates to see my suitcase rolling through the house on Sundays – he knows it means Dad will soon be gone for days. I'm surprised he doesn't attack it out of anger, but it's still a bit bigger than him – for now. I now expect that all the Marmaduke comic strips will be acted out in my house over the next few years.

Below is also a recent photo of Purty and our middle dog, Ranger in my home office (AKA the guest bedroom). There's also an old girl named Molly (a Shih Tzu), but she doesn't like to hang around Purt – he's just too big & rough for her refined tastes, and she's been whacked in the head by his formidable tail too many times.

Ranger tolerates Purt, but they don't roughhouse together anymore, since Purt almost cost him an eye. Purt either bit it in play or whacked it repeatedly with his tail, and a vet visit was necessary to intervene. After only a week plus $150, Ranger once again has binocular vision.

Purt recently made his own visit to the vet, to be "tutored" (a very old joke from a Far Side cartoon). We don't see any behavioral differences in him yet, but we certainly didn't want him to become even more aggressive (or affectionate, if you know what I mean...) than he already was. Fortunately, he was spared the "cone of shame", so he wasn't blundering about the house knocking over any more stuff than usual.

I didn't know this was possible, but Purty nearly scared one of our chickens to death last week. One morning, after putting him outside so the smaller dogs could eat breakfast, I found him in the fenced-off chicken yard, bent over an inert Polish rooster. I thought he had killed it, but my wife determined that it was only suffering from shock. (I wonder if it saw a bright light, and maybe a vision of Col. Sanders?)

Once again, I told my long-suffering wife that we could give Purty away if we needed to, and once again she told me to shush (several times, because I kept trying to finish my sentence). She knows what a softie I am, and how attached I've become to this lovable pain in the butt. But she's the one who has to deal with him while I'm on the road.

This last weekend, Purt climbed onto the chaise lounge behind me and explored my head, making me giggle like a 6-year old – and nothing has made me giggle like that for a long time. Of course, every time he gets up on the couch, he leaves a coating of sand, moisture, and hair behind, which means I have to vacuum the couch again. In fact, I looked up the meaning of the word "purt" today (to see if his name means anything, in any language) and it turns out to be American Urban slang for "pure dirt" – yep, that's him!

A friend from church told me when I got Purt that, "A dog will just break your heart when he dies!". But, as Vision says to Ultron at the end of the 2nd Avengers movie, "A thing isn't beautiful because it lasts." Purt's a big dog, and I realize that big dogs don't live as long as small ones.

But I'll enjoy my buddy "for as long as we both shall live" – and he may outlast me!

The extended family on Joce's side – love my bonus people!

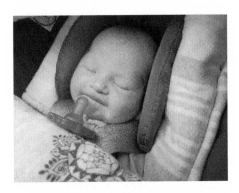

Our new niece, Josie Faith – and Uncle Kent is in love...

I Believe in People

As I travel around the USA (and now the world), I get to meet all kinds of folks. Most of those I meet are trainees in the classes I teach, but I also meet lots of hotel staff, wait staff, cab drivers, and airline attendants. Getting acquainted with these people is the best part of my job.

I believe that the way we treat those we meet reflects whatever's going on inside us. You may have heard of executives who judge those under them by how they treat wait staff with whom they interact. In other words, their character is judged by how they treat those who hold no power over them. Regardless of who's watching, I want to treat others well.

So, here's what I believe about those with whom I become acquainted:

1. Everyone deserves respect. In fact, I call everyone "sir" or "ma'am", but that's just a personal preference. I also show respect by learning names, and using them whenever appropriate.

2. Everyone is just a person, trying to get through his/her day or week. No matter how high up (or humble) a person is, he/she still has struggles, fears, and weaknesses. Remember, Superman is only a comic book character.

3. People desperately need to laugh, even if they're laughing at me! As a trainer, I love telling jokes. Folks do usually laugh, and sometimes they're laughing that I have the nerve to tell such a dumb joke. That's OK – they just need to laugh, because life is often hard.

4. I have no idea what's going on in the life of each person I meet. Some folks are dealing with unimaginable struggles, and they don't need me to add to those.

5. I must be generous. My wife reminds me that an extra dollar added to the tip means little to us, but can mean a great deal to a service person. A proverb I'm trying to live by states, "The generous man always has enough." I try to be generous with forgiveness, praise, and listening, too.

6. People can tell if I genuinely like them, and that greatly influences whether or not they like me. After all, we are most often drawn to those who we believe like us, however

different from us those people may seem. I do like most people I meet, and that's what makes my job so much fun!

Yes, the coolest thing about my job is meeting people. I've gotten to travel to NYC, Alaska, Curaçao, Las Vegas, Trinidad, Puerto Vallarta, and many other places, and I've seen lots of neat things, but it's the relationships that have the most value – it's the investment in others that counts. People are more fascinating, more memorable, and more important than any roller coaster, beach, skyscraper, or meal, so be good to those in your path today – they're important!

Friends around the bonfire – I didn't light it!

Let Me Introduce You...

My Dad – later in life, I called him "Papa". He's been gone from this earth for something over 7 years now, but I still see him, and hear him. And I think I feel him in my joints when I get up in the morning. I see him in the mirror, when I notice my jowls and the slightly bemused look in my eyes. I hear him when I tell our teenager some "Dad" thing Ben needs to hear.

I have some tapes of Papa's sermons, but I haven't been able to listen to any of them yet. For a couple of years, I had the excuse that we just didn't have a cassette player any longer – everything was on CD (or digital). But now the real issue is plain: I just don't want to face the pain of hearing the voice that never got to tell me he was proud of my Master's degree, that he's so proud that I have a wife who truly values me, or that I'm a good Dad – all things I've gained since he moved on.

Papa was a kind man, especially after old age softened him a bit. But he was always tender-hearted. He was a Pastor all my life – for the last 25 years before he retired, in Mesquite, and for a few years before that, in Sherman, TX. We came from Southern Illinois, and he (with my amazing Mama) pastored congregations from 6 to a few hundred, all over Illinois and Southern Michigan.

One of my earliest memories of Dad was him scaring me from the pulpit, pounding his fist on it as he thundered against sin, hell, and rebellion against God's way of life. I decided that God must sound like my Dad, with a big voice and a healthy supply of anger. But when Dad gave an altar call, his voice was inviting, compassionate, and close to breaking - to walk away was a terrifying tragedy.

I remember many times hearing him complain about how particular members were disappointing him by their lifestyles – unwilling to let go of habits that kept them from a deep love life with God, trapped by bad decisions, or simply skipping attendance at church. I thought he was just ticked off at these folks, until I came in one evening to find him praying for one of them, weeping as he knelt at a kitchen chair.

And I continue to marvel at how he established a family with God at its core, when the family in which he was raised was so different. His dad was a physically and verbally abusive heathen, who actually beat my grandmother for taking their kids (and dollars) to church. I remember that, because of how his dad "disciplined", Dad was hesitant to spank his own kids, because he was worried his temper would cause him to go too far. To my mind, he wasn't hesitant enough, though – I still had occasion to experience the force of his belt on my bottom (but not as much as I deserved).

As I write this, a day before Halloween, I'm on my last day as a 55-year-old man. For many years before losing Papa, I used to actually dread the phone call from my parents during which they'd sing *Happy Birthday* to me. It was tedious, and felt kind of silly to my adult ears. Wanna know how much I'd pay to have both my parents sing it to me tomorrow?

Not sure why Dad was wearing a crown...

Facets

(Note: this is the introduction to a book I've been writing about Heaven - for about 20 years. I hope to finish it in 2020)

A Boy and his Boy

They run, one with long, strong strides, seeming to sail across the ocean of deep green meadow. The other runs with steps so quick that his shorter legs blur. One is sometimes gone from sight for a moment, but the other can still feel him, hear him.

The breathing of both is intense and strong; one breathes deeply, taking strength with each inhalation; exhaling exhilaration. The other pants, his tongue cooling him as he flies along close to the ground. He occasionally explodes in joyous noise to his taller companion. Words are not necessary; the love is plain.

This is great play. The man suddenly veers to the left to run a circle around his companion of so many years, teasing him with mock slaps to the flank. The dog joins

142

in the game, trying to run his own circle around the boy he loved for his whole life.

They have found each other again, after how long? The dog doesn't know time; the man vaguely recalls that he was without his old friend for a while... before. But that doesn't matter now.

They both run on until the man stops to sit under a spreading oak. They aren't tired, but it feels good to rest. The dog curls up at his feet as he sits with his back against the wide trunk. They both laugh, in their own ways.

Dinner Party

Never on earth has there been a display of so much food of so many kinds. The tables are scattered over several thousand acres. Each table holds a different type of food. On one are hundreds of deep-dish pizzas in every variety. Another holds nachos, stuffed jalapeno peppers, sizzling fajita meat, and huge bowls of guacamole.

There are tables of German food, French crepes, Castilian seafood. Greek, Hebrew,

and other Mediterranean varieties fill an
acre. There's a hibachi grill with an angelic
cook who does miracles with his knives, to
the delight of his anticipating audience.

The guests wander from area to area,
stopping to sample this or that. Sometimes
they spot someone they haven't seen for a
long time, or someone they always wanted
to meet. Then there are hugs, backslaps,
kisses; whatever feels right. They stand
and converse; happily, deeply, fully.

Sometimes people decide to move to the
couches arranged in conversation pits
below the main floor. There are lots of
groups of people down there; laughing,
discussing, getting acquainted and re-
acquainted. Whether or not they knew
each other - "before", they know now – and
this takes time. Each person shares his or
her deepest longings and joys with another
person, sometimes with a group. Animated
discussions are going on all around;
discussions of turning points in history,
marvels of creation, the wonders of HIM.

Some people make other use of the
couches – they're peacefully napping. With

great satisfaction, those who had known so little satisfaction "before" put down their plates and cups, stretch their legs, sigh contentedly, and lie down for a snooze. Some sleep for days – not because they're so tired, but just because they *can*. No one's running late, no time spent here is deducted from anyone's allotment – everything can wait.

The people are quite a mixed bag; there are men with rich, white, flowing beards and hair who look strong, fit, and very alive. They move slowly but purposefully through the huge crowd. Often someone comes up to them shouting in recognition, and they're peppered with handshakes, hugs, and questions. They answer the questions, return the affection, and ask questions of their own.

They smile beatifically at young girls who seem about to burst with joy and excitement; running around animatedly, talking a mile a minute about who they've met, what they've seen, what their plans are for the next hours, days, weeks.

And HE is moving through the crowd; stopping as a young man rushes up to fall at His feet, embracing His ankles, weeping with joy and thanks. Tears fall like little rivers from the young man's eyes, bathing the Master's feet and puddling beneath them. The words are few; the young man is raised to his feet by one strong arm, then wrapped in both arms, and welcomed – home.

The Concert

The stage is <u>huge</u>; at least 100 yards across. It has several levels; connected by stairs, catwalks, and spirals. It's covered in instruments of every kind ever known, and others never seen before. There is a huge pipe organ, keyboard stacks, a grand piano; drums of steel, skin, and wood. Ram's horns, trumpets, and saxophones join violins, cellos, and harps. But there are no wires, no microphones, and no speakers.

Darkness like dusk suddenly descends – but there is no stage lighting. The audience hushes expectantly, and a lone spotlight suddenly shines on the front of the stage. A small woman with glory in her hair steps into the circle of light and begins to sing, "Great is Thy Faithfulness".

Her voice is strong, clear, and impassioned – it's obvious that she learned well His constancy. The sound carries throughout the vast assembly without need for amplification. They hear her, feel her, see the experiences in her song. Tears are flowing down her cheeks, but the song continues just as strong.

As the last note echoes, HE appears beside her. She falls on her face in front of The Lamb, and He raises her with a gesture. He thanks her, and she dances off the stage – without bothering with the stairs. He turns and is suddenly gone again.

Now a group of young men in their twenties takes the stage. They run the gamut of clothes and hair. One with a blonde mane cascading down his back moves to the front of the band as it assembles. He just stands there and beams at the crowd for a moment – then he screams, "I love you, Jesus!".

The rest of the guys find their instruments. They're giddy, each one like a child unwrapping the best present ever. They can't wait to try out these new toys.

A deep red electronic rhythm kit surrounds the drummer as he sits. The set responds to his wishes, each drum changing tones at his expectation. He leads off with a driving beat, then he stands and moves forward. The drums part in front of him and move with him, staying just close enough that they're all in his reach.

The lead guitar comes in next; an eight-stringed green metal wonder with seemingly limitless range and sustain. As with the drums, the tones produced by the guitar change according to the feeling of the musician, without any need for pedals or stomp boxes.

The bass is a six-stringed translucent purple model; headless and fretless. Its player flows into and around the rest of the music, buoying it up. Keyboards round out the mix, decorating the song where no one knew there was any room left. The singer is blasting now, with unheard-of range, glorifying God as he jumps around the stage in seven-foot arcs.

Each musician does more than he ever thought possible, going beyond the previously-known range of himself and his instrument. When the song is done, the Lion appears once more, thanking each guy for the wonderful song. He disappears again, and a dignified-looking gentleman steps up to the pipe organ.

He sits down on a padded bench, looks up at the pipes, and smiles – they range from a few inches long to over 100 feet. The keyboards comprise six levels, surrounding the bench on three sides. There are three levels of foot pedals. Johann Sebastian Bach smiles with anticipation, then begins to play, "Ode to Joy" – to Joy Himself.

He's followed by a bluegrass troupe, then a string quartet, then a man sitting on a stool playing an acoustic guitar while tears stream down his face. There's a steel-drum band, mariachis, and someone in kingly robes playing a lyre. A group of Zulu tribesmen appears, beating tree-trunks with skins stretched over them. They chant, "glory to The Lamb, glory to The Lamb, glory to the Lamb who was slain!". The languages are as different as the people, as different as the instruments, as different as the sound – and everyone understands perfectly.

Maggie

Maggie awakened to light flooding through a huge picture window. She looked at her feet, stretched out on the couch in front of her. "My", she thought, "this is a really big couch – my couch is small and saggy." She sat up and looked around the room, then wondered idly, "Where am I?"

She knew she had been asleep, but had she forgotten where she was? She reached for her glasses and couldn't find them. But then she realized that she could see everything clearly, both nearby and out the window. Her curiosity about this was overshadowed for the moment as she looked around the room.

The room she was in was larger than her whole apartment, and the picture window was larger than any of her walls. And the walls here were covered with pictures. The door – well, there was just an open doorway, and she noticed a warm breeze gently blowing through it, with the scent of some wonderful flower carried on it. She heard little girls' voices singing happily.

She could see three hallways leading off of the room she was in, and she felt a bit curious about where they went. Maybe she would explore this place in a little while. Maybe she'd figure out, or remember, what this place was.

Maggie got up from the couch and stretched – and then wondered aloud at how strong and... alive she felt. Why, there was no pain in any of her joints! She had just been prayed for up front at church last Sunday – she must have been healed again! And that would explain her clear eyesight, too! Praise God!

She even felt *taller*. That was strange – she'd never been very tall, and she knew that she had become stooped as she got older. But when she looked down at the floor, it certainly seemed to be farther away than she remembered. Maybe her eyes were playing tricks on her.

She went to look at the pictures on one wall – why, she was in this one! And, as she watched, the scene began to move, like a tiny TV set. But the picture was as clear as the view out the window, and, as she listened, she could make out plainly the sounds coming from it.

This picture showed her, on her knees. Even without listening, she knew what this scene was – this was one of the many nights she had been praying for Franklin. He had been so wild, so angry and full of pain. Since she knew that God was powerful and she wanted the best for her son, she had decided to pray for what people thought was impossible – that Franklin would be saved, and that God would make him a <u>preacher</u>.

When he was 18, God finally got through to him, and soon after that he <u>was</u> called to preach. She still remembered his first sermon – he was so nervous, and his message was so short, but she was <u>so</u> proud of him, and even more thankful to the Lord. He was pastor of a church in Texas now, and lots of folks had been saved under his preaching over the years.

Other screens showed other things that had happened to her. The one on the next screen over was a movie of her coming home from a revival meeting with Franklin in tow, when he was only 10. Yes, she remembered this one too well... there was Robert at the door, cursing and threatening. He hated her going to church.

In the scene, Robert threw the door open and grabbed her arm. He dragged her inside and backhanded her in the face. He was strong from his years in the coal mines, and she fell hard, crying. Why did he do this to her?

She remembered the pain she had felt, but in the picture she noticed something else. When he hit her, something seemed to fly from her face – what looked like little golden snowflakes rose from every place she was hit, and kept rising until each one was captured by a beautiful person who floated (?!) over the scene.

When the beating stopped, there was something else she hadn't seen before – a majestic person stood before her as she lay crumpled on the floor. The glorious young man was tall enough that his head brushed the ceiling, and he nearly filled the small room with his bulk.

The man knelt down and poured something over her head. Some of what he poured seeped into her head, while the rest of it moved over all of her body and into it, right through her skin. In watching the scene now, Maggie could see something begin to grow inside her. It was like her spirit had gotten a big drink of water when it was very thirsty.

The last of it ran off of Maggie and filled the air inside their apartment. It hung there for a moment, then dissolved into the walls, floor, and ceiling. They were *glowing* from whatever it was. Then the picture changed back to the beginning of the scene.

She moved to the next picture. It showed her witnessing to a teenage boy on the street corner in downtown Alton. She handed him a gospel tract, and she told him in her simple way how much Jesus loved him. As she said the words to him, each one became a solid object resting on the boy. The words built up like snow on his head and shoulders.

This scene followed the boy home. He entered his room, sat down on the floor and read the tract she had given him. As he read, her words echoed in the air around him. He began to cry, and she saw his spirit stretch out to heaven in prayer.

The scene changed to a view of a throne, with someone Wonderful (!) sitting on it. As the boy's words echoed around the throne, they seemed to be the only thing anyone was listening to. The beautiful people around the throne suddenly started cheering and dancing. Some were blowing horns, some were flying around in circles, and others just fell facedown around the throne, with their heads pointing toward it...

More to come...

Unsafe at Any Speed

Driving two of "my munchkins" from the church to the local donut shop would have been much simpler if it had happened 50 years ago. They would have just piled into the bed of my truck, sitting down if they didn't want the wind to mess up their hair (these were 3- and 5-year-old girls). Of course, if they were boys, they'd just brace themselves against the cab and grin into the wind (A few junebugs never hurt anyone!). But those days are gone, and I even know a family who lost a son when he was thrown from a truck bed.

On this trip, my problem was rear-facing car seats – I don't own any. Having never had a little one (I became dad to a teen in my mid-50s), I've never owned a car seat. But the drive between our church and the donut shop is only about a mile, and our Youth Pastor decided that his daughters would be safe enough in my truck cab for that short a trip. I was extremely careful, and we made it there and back without incident – Whew!

That reminded me of my Dad's idea of "safety" when I was the same age as those girls. I remember sleeping in the rear deck window of our Oldsmobile, listening to the hum of the road as he drove 80 miles per hour on two-lane highways, passing nearly everyone in our lane. When I was through sleeping, I'd sometimes stand on the hump between the two rear floorboards, watching the road coming at me as I leaned forward to let it fill my field of vision. Dad's driving was always exciting.

"Exciting" driving became undesirable around Dad's 70th year – he really scared me driving a church van from Mesquite to downtown Dallas, and I vowed never again to ride in a vehicle he was driving. I took over on the drive home, and Dad was gracious about it, which surprised me. I've heard that losing driving privileges is one of the most painful changes an older person faces.

Riding with Papa in his 70s was a bit like riding with our son as I taught him to drive – I felt scared and powerless, stepping hard on an imaginary brake. Their issues with driving were totally opposite – Papa had too much confidence in aggressive driving skills that had degraded over time, while Ben had no skills and zero confidence.

As I've mentioned, we live on a dead-end country road. To help Ben gain some confidence as a driver, I had him drive down the middle of our street in my beat-up 1998 Ford Ranger. He was so nervous that he was physically shaking; in fact, he hit a neighbor's mailbox with the passenger-side mirror. But he eventually became a safer driver than me.

My drive to the donut shop with these precious little girls made them happy that day, and they might have remembered for a few days that "Mr. Kent" took them for a ride. But, to me, it was a precious chance to bless these little lives and make them feel special. And when their parents became pastors in Louisiana, I was so glad that I had that memory.

Their family's been gone for a couple of years now, and the last time I saw the girls, they didn't remember me. That's fine, because it's not about my significance; it's about theirs. I want them, and every little one with whom I interact, to understand his/her worth. Jesus said 'Let the little children come to me". They are important to Him, and if God says someone's important, well, they are!

This little angel helped us set up the 2019 Health Fair

Reader Response Response

Over the course of the months this column has been published, I have received e-mail responses from four readers (besides family members and church friends). The first one was "hate mail", which made me giddy – I sent excited text messages about it to my siblings and a close friend. I figured that if someone cared enough about what I wrote to send me a vitriolic message, I was a "real" writer!

Since then, I have received three positive responses, including one in which a reader thought I might need an "understanding ear". That one really touched me, because this man read between the lines of the column (about how my church helped me heal), and offered help. Though my life is very happy now, I can always use more friends, so I'm grateful to him.

I love to hear that others have laughed along with me at something ridiculous (like installing a car stereo on my tractor in 'Tractor Lust'), or have gotten the benefit of a lesson God is teaching me (like how unnecessary is my understanding - 'Pray for Monkeys'). I write primarily for my own amusement, and from my need to share meaning. I like imagine that I'm sitting in the same room with readers, telling a story.

One of my friends is in prison, and she shares with her friends there the clippings of my column I send every 2-3 weeks. So, I may very well be famous in the Texas penal system! I'm certainly not famous anywhere else, although another columnist for my hometown paper did approach me in the grocery store yesterday – she remarked that she enjoyed the funny columns I've written.

I've read that many writers consider humor to be more difficult to write than tragedy, maybe because this life has so many hardships. That's exactly the reason humor is so <u>important</u> – it helps balance our lives. And that's one reason I find it easy to poke fun at myself – I laugh at me, and I want others to get the benefit of it <u>with</u> me.

My column 'Blood, Sweat, and…" described my tendency to injure myself, but I also laugh at:

1. My obsessive sense of order about "my" kitchen. If the lady who cleans for us moves my salt or pepper, or puts a pan away in a

spot other than where I usually store it, I get very frustrated. But having this help makes it more likely my lovely wife will remain the sane person in our household, because Ben & I can't see dirt (it's a guy thing).

2. Fans & lights: fans only make a room feel cooler to a person in that room. Leaving a fan on when no one's in a room is wasteful. Of course, a ceiling fan left on costs an additional 50 cents per *decade*, sooooo... it's tough to make my case on this one.

3. Eating one thing at a time – yes, I'm one of those folks who eats all my fries before starting on the burger, all my peas before my hot dog, and all my salad before my baked beans. I think that's because I'm easily confused – I need to let my mouth become accustomed to one flavor before introducing another.

4. And... since 'Blood, Sweat, and ...' was published, I managed to drop a hatchet on my head (the blunt side, fortunately). The hatchet incident happened when I attempted to move a rolling ladder without first retrieving from the work platform the hatchet I'd been using – when the wheels

hit something, the ladder stopped rolling, but the hatchet continued on. My wife heard me yell and came over to investigate. At about the time I said, "I'm fine, just a little bump!", the blood started to trickle down my forehead.

So, please continue to respond – I love to hear from readers, whether you love or hate what I have to say... or if you're just want to know how I achieve such amazing crust on my BBQ chicken! My e-mail address is: sipeskent@gmail.com.

Overlooking the Badlands – where I was considering hiding out from the photographer

At the King's Ranch – pt. 1

If you've never played catch with a 12-year-old boy, you're missing a spectacular experience. Now, don't get the idea that I'm talking about tossing a baseball or football with a kid – no, I mean throwing a pre-teen through the air to another adult. Yes, I have done that, and yes, I do hope that the statute of limitations on child endangerment has passed (or expired, or whatever such statutes do when they die).

During the 2 years I worked for the King's Ranch in Morrow, AR, as a counselor, I had some quite interesting experiences. This one only happened when a neighbor invited us to bring the "Ranch boys" to swim in his pool. We happened to have a very undersized kid whom I'll call "Ronnie"; who was so small that I could lift him over my head and toss him to another counselor ("Steve") across the pool. If we'd only had a net, we could have played "human volleyball".

Ronnie pretended to be afraid as he flew through the air, arms flailing (his screams were pretty convincing). But I also think he liked the attention, and we "adults" saw this as a job perk (which is very sad; I know). Each of us earned all of $100/week; barely enough for me to pay for my car and 1 fun outing on my day off each Thursday (usually a Chinese or pizza buffet, plus a few dollars for the arcade (this was in the late 1980s). And I'm happy to report that Ronnie lived!

Working at "The Ranch" was an unforgettable experience. When I first visited the facility to see if I would be a good fit, I stepped outside the first night and saw the stars more vividly than I had ever seen them before - I was in love. In the foothills of the Ozarks, in a town of 200, there's not much "light pollution", and a canopy of stars, horizon to horizon, is the result.

Anyway, I took the position when the Director offered it, and set a time a few weeks in the future as my first "official" day with the Ranch. My home church gave me a nice send-off, complete with gifts to help me get started as a "home missionary". I imagine that some of them were happy to see me find a role that might allow me to blossom, and they were tired of putting up with "the Pastor's rowdy son".

Since we earned so little, I decided I could look however I wanted, and didn't cut my hair (in back) for over a year. I kept the front in a flattop; in fact, one stylist there in AR even cut my hair using a level. I grew a beard, too, but that was just pitiful – I can't grow enough facial hair to accomplish anything but making my face look out-of-focus. And I wore bib overalls when the weather was cool – just going for the whole "ignorant yokel" look.

Some of the best and worst experiences of my life happened at the King's Ranch. I lived in the most beautiful country I'd ever seen, I made some great friends, and I managed to grow my hair down over my shoulders. And then there was the night I was awakened at 1 AM and informed that two of the boys had stolen my car.

"It was the best of times; it was the worst of times". I'll write more about The Ranch later, unless I get some complaints (in which case I'll probably write about the complaints – see *Reader Response Response*).

I'm so grateful for the chance to share my life with y'all, and, every once in a while, I hear from a reader via e-mail (Fans – 6;

Hate Mail – 1) – that means we're having a real conversation!

One of our students at the Ranch drew caricatures of the staff... what an interesting group!!

Seldom is Heard an Encouraging Word

Mark Twain once said that he could go a week on a good compliment – how about you? Are you being recognized for the great things you do at work? And what about the people around you – are they being recognized for their contributions?

Most people would say that they don't get enough positive recognition. And, while you may not be able to change the amount of "good press" that you receive in the short run, there is something you can do to improve your work environment in the long run. If you will become a source of sincere positive recognition, some of that recognition is bound to make its way back to you.

Here are some tips on how to be an effective "person-builder":

1. Specific praise – instead of just saying "Good job today!", effective praise is specific, such as, "I noticed how you went out of your way to make sure that customer's problem was solved, then followed up to make sure he was happy!".

2. Sincere – if you can, look that person in the eye when you are speaking to him/her. Use simple words, and don't be flowery or overly dramatic. Just say what you have to say and let it be over.

3. In public – I used to work for Mary Kay, and one of her hallmark phrases was "Praise in public, discipline in private." In other words, let other people hear when you say something good to someone about his/her actions.

4. Gossip – along with telling the person who did the good work about his/her good work, consider also telling someone *else* about the good thing you saw a co-worker do. Don't we all need to hear more about the good things that happen at work?

5. Look for things to recognize – do you ever feel "unnoticed" for the effort you put in every day? Don't you think that your co-workers sometimes feel that way as well? How about the checkout person at your supermarket – does he/she ever feel that way? If you work at it just a little, you can become a pretty good "person-builder".

6. Sandwich theory – another thing Mary Kay practiced was to surround with positive comments any corrective comments she needed to give an employee. If she was discussing with an employee an issue that needed to change, she first mentioned something positive she'd noticed or heard about that employee, then the negative comment, then another positive comment.

7. Big shot - remember that the people who are in positions of authority are just people too! Those folks need to hear the good things they do, just like everyone else does. Often, that person in authority is burdened with responsibilities and conflicting priorities that the rest of us don't understand. Don't flatter him/her, but don't be afraid to sincerely mention the good things that you've noticed about him/her or about his/her work.

If you'll begin today to practice this, you'll be surprised at how positively people react, and how much you enjoy it. A few years ago, I mentioned to a flight attendant how professionally she took care of a bunch of crowded fliers. She told me that "made her day"! Obviously, it didn't take much to vastly improve her enjoyment of her work.

As this "people-building" becomes more normal in your daily interactions, you'll become very good at spotting what's good in others. And there's a Bible proverb that says, "He who refreshes others will be himself refreshed." I think that means someone's gonna point out what's going right with you!

Shameless plug for my wife's therapy practice in Tyler, Texas

Top 10 Ways to Know You're an Effective Salesperson

1. Your voice mail can only be reached via a "900" number.

2. Your Sales Manager organizes a weekly lottery in which 5 lucky customers get to take you to lunch.

3. Phone calls from customers routinely begin with "I'll take 12 of them!".

4. You cut back your work schedule to 1 day a week to avoid being bumped into a higher tax bracket - it doesn't work.

5. Customers often send you their platinum cards with notes that read "Just send me whatever you think I need."

6. Customers hotly debate whether or not it's better to let you win at golf.

7. Your Sales Manager comes over each Saturday to mow your lawn and take car of other household chores because "You need your rest."

8. Customers hear that you're ill and call to ask if one of their kidneys will help.

9. The "Salesperson of the Month" parking space is permanently engraved with your name.

10. Your company issues a memo to your customers requesting that they stop sending Christmas gifts - the storage facility is full.

Top 10 Ways to Know You're an Ineffective Salesperson

 1. You finally make a sale and your company bookkeeper deletes the order as a "data entry error".

2. You have to stop making prospecting calls because you run out of quarters.

3. Your office doubles as the janitorial closet.

4. Security guards at your sales appointments confiscate the donuts you brought and have your car towed from their parking lot.

5. Rumors of your impending retirement cause your company's stock price to triple.

6. Your co-workers try to convince you that the weekly sales meeting has been moved to the Denny's parking lot at 1:30 AM Saturday.

7. Prospects return your calls just so they can scream "NO! NO! A thousand times, NO!!!" into the phone.

8. Your Sales Manager often leaves brochures for the "Jack In The Box Management Training Program" in your mailbox.

9. Your son refuses your help at his lemonade stand because "You just don't have the performance history he's looking for."

10. Your company vehicle is downgraded from "moped" to "skateboard".

Feeling fierce (just before I hurt my back)

This is a blank page. Just as in the 1st book (*Thank You, my Friends – the 5-year Plan*), all articles begin on a right-facing page, meaning that some pages, like this one, contain absolutely nothing. That's right, a totally blank page.

So, if you have young children who enjoy scribbling in your books, this page is the perfect opportunity for them to exercise their creativity. Rest assured, I did not place these white pages in the book simply to expand its length, but only to increase its readability – no one is paying me by the word for my humorous writing.

Of course, I only know of one person in particular who "gets" my humor – a kind lady who carries out my groceries at the local Brookshire's (Hi, Jean!). Jean tells me that she has read at least one of the entries in my 1st book (*The Fish Head is Staring at Me!*) five times. Doubtless, Jean is very short of reading materials in her restroom, where I imagine this book is kept (the pages are too stiff to use for other "bathroom purposes").

So, anyway, this blank page is only here to satisfy my habit of many years, as a Technical Writer, to begin sections on a

Top 10 Ways to Know your Training is Effective:

10. Your training director refers to you as "O exalted one, keeper of all wisdom."

9. During a business downturn, your CEO cuts her own position to avoid cutting yours.

8. Students vote to form a new religion based on your training.

7. Students routinely camp out in front of your training center for several days before class begins to ensure they'll get a good seat.

6. The surviving Beatles, Julian Lennon, and Yoko Ono unite to record an album based on your teachings.

5. Third World nations have <u>your</u> picture on their currencies.

4. Students beg permission to name <u>all</u> their children after you.

3. Scalpers (unsuccessfully) offer to trade students 50-yard line Super Bowl tickets for admission to your class.

2. Sports Illustrated cancels its annual swimsuit edition in order to devote that month's coverage to you.

1. Students have to be reassured that they won't miss anything by occasionally blinking.

I've also taught Spanish

PawPaw & Joyce ("Sir & Mrs. Sir") – I married Joce & got them as a bonus!

Top 10 Ways to Know your Training is Ineffective:

10. Not only do students fail to return from the lunch break, they attempt to flee the country.

9. An argument ensues about who most deserves everlasting torment: you, Charles Manson or Adolf Hitler. You win.

8. You resort to giving illegal drugs as prizes for class participation.

7. The most popular coffee additive in your class is hemlock.

6. A student who suffers a stroke during your class thereafter carries the nickname of "Lucky."

5. Your training director offers to trade you to office support for two temps and a used mimeograph.

4. The most frequent comment heard in your class is, "Huh?"

3. After three days of training, you realize

that the students speak only <u>Norwegian</u>.

2. Students take up a collection to have a hit put out on you.

1. Students refer to your half-day seminar as "Hell Week."

The only tractor I currently own

Top 10 Ways to Spot a Bad Consultant

1. Consultant will not acknowledge any question posed to him unless prefaced by the phrase "O, Exalted One, in whom resides all pertinent data..."

2. Resume highlights include "Guitar Hero 3" and "Grand Theft Auto" scores.

3. Tip jar on her desk includes a small card listing suggested "donation" amounts, based on the complexity of the client's questions.

4. Typical response to client questions about recommendations is, "Because I said so, and I'm the Consultant!!! Thus saith the Consultant. You may be excused."

5. Instead of showing up at the client site on Monday morning, consultant sends a cardboard cutout of himself sitting in a chair with his back turned. No one notices any difference.

6. Claims to travel to client site via astral projection while her body remains at an espresso bar.

7. Client references include names such as "Johnny the Shank" and "Fat Tony" - client locations limited to state and federal prisons.

8. Bills client for 320 hours of work done by his multiple personalities during a one-week period.

9. 50-mile trip from consultant's home to client site generates 1200 frequent-flier miles.

10. Knowledge transfer from consultant to client involves secret handshake and muttered phrases in Sanskrit.

Purty Puppy

We recently added a new member to our clan (*This is an old article*), and I named him "Purt". Don't ask me why I chose that name; it just came to me, though I tell folks around here it's because he's "gonna be purty big" and "He's a purty puppy, ain't he?". Right now he's smaller than our other three dogs (Mollie, an elderly female Shih Tzu, Ranger, a male Boston Terrier mix, and Scrappy, a Chihuahua street dog my wife adopted), but we expect him to be bigger than the three of them combined (75-100#).

We adopted him from a family in our church, based on three qualifications: 1. We could acquire him at no cost.   2. He was a male (we boys like to roughhouse).   3. He seemed to like us. To determine which puppy "liked us", we reached into the "male" side of the cage to see which clamored to be picked up. We then picked up the most fervent puppies, determined which were most "licky", then lowered them to the ground and watched for which ones stayed close. Purt passed each test, and he had a distinctive white blaze on his chest and neck, while the rest were totally black.

Purt is the product of a Giant Schnauzer male and a Boxer female, both good-natured adults. He, on the other hand, seems intent only on:

A. Using his ultra-sharp puppy teeth on us

B. Trying to entice the other three dogs to play with him.

Being the "Dad", I sometimes let him chew on my arm or my finger, until I notice I'm bleeding, at which point I try to make him stop biting. This means that I must either provide something other than my body for him to chew on, or place him on the floor.

Placing Purt on the floor means he will once again try to entice the other dogs to play-fight, eliciting growls from two of the three. He has managed to draw the most playful, Ranger, into scuffling with him about once a day. The other two just growl and snap at his "attacks", especially old Molly, whose tail Purt believes to be a totally different creature than her head. He always seems surprised when he paws at the tail and the head spins around and snaps at the air in front of him.

Purt enjoys chasing the chickens around the yard. He has yet to catch one, but, to him, they seem to be animated toys placed there just for him. I don't think he'd know what to do if he caught one. There's little danger of that right now, since they're all bigger than he is. We expect that to be true for about two more weeks.

Biting is just his way of experiencing the world through his mouth, sort of like a food critic – but Purt's much less choosy about what he takes in… and I'll leave it at that. We bought him puppy food, and it all gets eaten soon after I put it out – but Purt doesn't eat it; he prefers the adult hi-pro (expensive) dog food. The other dogs love his puppy chow, though – seems fair.

We plan to make him a yard dog, but I'm having second thoughts about that – he whines whenever he's out in the yard, wanting (I suppose) to be with the people and the inside dogs. My wife's pretty soft-hearted, so maybe if he and I both look pitiful, Purt will be an inside dog… or maybe she'll just send me to sleep outside and keep him company.

When we got Purt, he fit pretty easily in my hand. As I close this article, he barely fits in my forearm and hand, legs spilling out. He doesn't know what to do with his giant feet, and often trips over them (like me!).

But after he torments the other dogs, and he's worn out, he sleeps the totally relaxed puppy sleep, dreaming of chasing chickens and thrashing toilet paper rolls. It's pretty sweet, especially when he's sleeping on my lap, barking little dream peeps, moving his big black paws, then stretching to get comfortable again, before heading back to slumberland. What a precious lot of trouble he is...

Purt was this size for... a few hours?

I _Was_ the Dad...

Our son is going to college. His serious medical issues (loss of vision, cataplexy) delayed him for a semester, but, as I write this, he's taking an entrance test at a nearby junior college. He even plans to live on campus, and I suspect that I'm part of the reason he's moving out. Two men in one house (even one as big as our farmhouse) usually means conflict.

And that's the way it's supposed to be. Like baby birds pushed out of the nest, young men need space to discover their passions and focus their dreams. We probably didn't help push him much when we remodeled his room, replacing the gross, 30-year-old carpet with Pergo and painting the walls and ceiling some shade of greyish-green (think dried seaweed).

As I've written ('Being the Dad'), I've seen "the boy" progress from a pre-teen couch potato to a 6' 3" couch potato with sideburns.

No, I'm just kidding – he's not so lazy anymore. When his mom and I married a bit over 4 years ago, we all began cleaning up our 3-acre property (it had been largely abandoned for 6 years before we bought it). I'm pretty strong, but lifting the trunk of a dead tree into the bonfire was a 2-man job. Besides helping me lift many heavy things, he has:

- Made several runs to the scrapyard to sell off some of what was left by the previous owner.

- Mowed our front yard with a human-powered "reel" mower

- Bathed all our dogs (we've had up to 4 at once) innumerable times

- Changed overhead light bulbs (I think our house will just eventually go dark when he's not around)

- Fetched (Ha!) dog treats from the top shelf of our kitchen cabinets (since he's by far the tallest person in our household)

- Performed aluminum can recycling, dishwasher loading/unloading, assorted chicken duties, and trash duties week after week

191

- Walked across bed frames as he helped me rotate our King-sized mattress

- Delivered my daily "chocolate surprises" to his Mama when I'm on the road.

Now that the prospect of him being gone is real, his mom gets a bit weepy about it once in a while. We're wondering what to do with his room – I voted for a game room (regulation air hockey table, foosball, ping-pong, chessboard). My wife voted for exercise room (Bowflex, treadmill, Olympic weight set)….. So, anyway, I think we'll really <u>enjoy</u> our new exercise room!

Having been a Dad for only a few years, I feel a bit cheated that my time was so short. The teen years were tough on all of us, but watching him choose his schedule of classes, I felt immensely proud of him, and grateful that I got to be the "Bonus Dad" for a while. Of course, I'm not abdicating my "Dad" role, but his growing independence means a change in our relationship – I'll no longer be his disciplinarian, taskmaster, and fitness coach; but, hopefully, his friend.

And before he goes, we're gonna make one last pass through the house looking for dead overhead bulbs.

Thanksgiving, with Papa at the head of the table

Miracles I Have Witnessed or in which I Have Been Involved

Rev. William F. Sipes *(as edited by Kent Sipes)*

1. The earliest miracle in our family was that my sister Gracie, born weighing two pounds, three ounces, lived without the benefit of an incubator. Though I was a child, I grew up aware of this. She was so small she slept in a drawer, and was quite sickly - she had pneumonia one year, double pneumonia the next year, and pneumonia again the following year. This so weakened her lungs that she contracted advanced tuberculosis.

   X-rays showed her lungs to be so infected that she was ordered to be placed in a sanatorium in Edwardsville, IL. My mother was heartbroken at the thought of placing her baby in this institution for a year or more. The X-rays showing the lung damage were taken on a Friday, and Grace was to be isolated on the following Monday.

We were attending Edwards St. Assembly of God church in Alton, IL (now called "Abundant Life"), and on the Sunday before Grace was to be isolated, my mother took her before the congregation for special prayer. I was six or seven years old at the time, and Grace was about three years old.

When Mother took Grace to the sanatorium on Monday, she insisted that the doctors take another X-ray. They thought she was crazy, but she insisted – she <u>knew</u> that Gracie had been healed. And the X-rays proved she was right.

They showed evidence of scarring from the areas infected by the TB, but there was no longer tuberculosis present. There was no need to institutionalize the child, because her chest and lungs were completely healed.

2. At age 12, while riding down a steep hill in a coaster wagon, I went over an embankment and dropped about 10 feet. Both bones in my right arm were broken just above the wrist and my elbow was totally dislocated. My father carried me to

the doctor, whom he later said had been drunk.

My arm was placed in a cast and sling, and after a number of weeks the cast was removed. There was a lump on the inside of my arm at the elbow which the doctor tried to pass off as normal. However, I knew something was wrong, because my arm wasn't working normally. Mother took me before the church for anointing and prayer.

I forgot about any problems with the arm and began to play baseball and other sports. At about 15 years of age, I began to lift weights in order to build up my body. I also began to pitch fast-pitch softball at age 15 or 16, and played basketball and football (although never well enough to earn a school letter). I was never very good at anything but baseball and softball, but I played those sports on two or three teams during a season.

At times my arm would hurt for a while, but the pain would soon go away. A number of years later, I experienced pain while working at Sears, Roebuck, & Co. in Alton, IL. The store sent me to see Dr. Mira, who took X-rays of the arm. I told him the story of how the arm was broken and dislocated, and how I believed my mother's prayers had resulted in the healing of my arm.

He said that was fine, but that he didn't believe in such things. I told him that I believed the bones were crossed in my arm – set incorrectly for many years, and that one bone was out of socket at the elbow. He sneered and said that was impossible – if that were true, I would have no use of that arm.

A day or so later, he called to tell me that he had the results of the X-rays, and that they showed exactly what I believed – the bones were crossed and one bone was out of socket at the elbow. He said that "Mother Nature" had created muscle to take the place of bone – very strange.

He also asked if I would permit him to use my X-rays in a presentation at an orthopedic conference in Chicago. I agreed, but before he hung up I testified again to the healing power of God that I knew I had personally witnessed.

3. The miracle that probably affected me most as a young man of 16 or 17 concerned a young deaf girl by the name of Mary. Every year there was a union tent revival in the Alton, IL area, which was our home. Evangelists such as O.L. Jaggers, A.A. Allen, Robert Fierro, and David Nunn would be invited by the Assemblies of God churches in the area. These men were used by God in healing throughout the world.

I can still recall the night that Mary went forward for prayer. After the evangelist had prayed for her ears, he asked her if she could hear him, and she said "Yes". He stepped behind her and whispered her name, and she turned around at the sound.

I was transfixed because Mary was someone I knew personally, and I knew she was deaf. I had to verify for myself that she had been healed. I was skeptical – I wanted to believe, because I had seen other miracles but was still not totally persuaded of their existence.

I crept around the outside of the tent to where Mary was standing, and softly called her name from behind. She abruptly turned around in response to my call. I could not handle this experience, and ran off crying, knowing for myself that God was real and I had just witnessed a miracle. Its effect has never left me.

4. As a young pastor in my first full-time pastorate in Robinson, IL, I began to experience breathing problems. The problems became increasingly worse, and it became difficult to sleep at night - I lay awake trying to breathe. Many nights were spent in my recliner, where I tried to survive.

Two or three times each week, I went to a local clinic for breathing treatments. I began to take medication and using inhalers. I took increasingly larger pills to control my symptoms, and I grew increasingly asthmatic. I was told that I might have to leave the ministry, but I knew this was not God's will for my life.

By this time I was pastoring in Granite City, IL, where evangelist David Nunn was holding a revival. I went forward for prayer, as I had done many times. I had been prayed for by other preachers, by my deacons, and by my friends. But I knew that this time something was different.

There had been no cold chills, hot flashes, or bolts of lightning, but I knew I had been healed. I told my wife, Wanda, that I was healed. I took the pills I stored in the window over the kitchen sink and used the spray attachment to wash them down the drain. I never took another pill for asthma, and I never again experienced another asthmatic attack.

I went on to compete heavily in sports, especially four-wall handball. I passed senior lifesaving at the local YMCA, ran a mile or two each day, and played basketball. Whenever someone asked me why I played so hard, I shared what God had done. This gave me great joy and an opportunity to share the news of God's healing power.

5. At one time, I pastored Bellemore Assembly of God church in Granite City, IL. Part of my congregation were youngsters from one family who were sometimes accompanied by their mother. Their father worked at a

job that resulted in oil and tar stains on his overalls, which their mother would often treat with gasoline before putting them in the washer.

However, once when she did this something (possibly a spark from the washer or dryer) ignited the gasoline on the clothes. As she dropped the clothes, the fire began to envelope the washroom. She and her husband attempted to extinguish the fire, but could not. They quickly vacated the house, along with all of their children – or so they believed.

The husband looked around and found that one child was unaccounted-for. By this time, the fire had engulfed the entire house. But the father ran back inside the house, trying unsuccessfully to locate the missing child. (He did not know that the child had left the house by a different route.) The father stayed in the burning house too long, and had to be rescued.

He was burned over 85% of his body. His Achilles tendon was completely destroyed, and he was in critical condition. There was little hope that he would live.

I went to the hospital in East St. Louis, IL to see him. As I entered the floor on which the burn unit was located, I was immediately assaulted by the smell of burnt flesh. When I arrived at his room, the nurse stationed outside the door asked who I was, and I explained that I pastored the church his children attended. She said she would allow me to step inside the room to pray for him, but that he probably would not live through the night.

I put a mask over my nose and mouth and stepped inside. The stench was so overwhelming that I felt as if I would throw up. I steeled myself to the smell and looked at a white man burned black. Tears came to my eyes. I said to the Lord, "Father, they say he can't live, and if he did live, he would never walk again. I'm asking you to perform a miracle. I ask in Jesus' name that you heal this man as a testimony to his family that our God is able to heal to the uttermost."

As I walked out of the room, the nurse entered. As I was disposing of my paper mask and gown, she came back out and told me that his vital signs showed that he didn't have long to live. I smiled and walked away, knowing in my spirit that God had heard me and healed him.

Five months later, this man who wasn't expected to live, and would definitely never walk again, walked into my church with his family. Using a cane for support, he stood and gave God the glory.

6. While holding a revival in Bunker Hill, IL, God did a remarkable miracle. In fact, the pastor, Frank Fuente, said that he had never seen anything like it. I had preached that night on deliverance from habits that had "shackled" people. Primarily I addressed those with alcohol, tobacco, and illicit drug habits.

As soon as I gave the altar call, the front of the church became filled with those seeking deliverance from habits. A number of those were people who had asked Christ into their lives but were still chained to smoking tobacco. One was my wife's uncle, John Martin.

As I began to pray and lightly touch people (without any force or pushing by me), they began to fall as if they had been hit by a sledgehammer. No one had to catch them, and no one was hurt. The people were lying everywhere. The church was packed that night, so it was quite a scene.

There were 13 people who later stood to testify that they had been delivered from the use of tobacco (mostly smokers). From that day on, John Martin never smoked again. He declared that he had no more desire to smoke.

However, that's not the end of the story. Many years later, as my wife, Wanda, and I were crossing a parking lot in Yellowstone Park, in Wyoming, someone loudly called my name. A couple on the other end of the lot called to me again, and started toward us. I said to my wife, "Do you know who they are?", and she replied that she did not.

By that time, they had made their way over to us. The woman said, "You don't remember us, do you?". I replied that I was sorry, but I did not remember them. She told me that they had been in a revival meeting I had held in Bunker Hill, IL some number of years before, and that her husband was one of those delivered that night.

God is still delivering people.

7. While attending Great Lakes Bible Institute (GLBI) in Zion, IL, I was asked to sing for the wedding of Gerald Royce, a close friend. The wedding was to take place in his hometown of White Lake, WI. I don't remember what was wrong with the car I was driving at the time, but I knew it could not make the round trip.

    I mentioned this to another friend, Guy Stambaugh, who owned a big '98 Oldsmobile. Oldsmobile made an '88 model and a '98 model. The '98 was much larger and heavier than the '88.

    During this time in our lives, finances were very tight. I filled the big gas tank, and knew I had enough gas to get from GLBI to Wisconsin. Gerald had promised to pay me $20 for driving to his wedding to sing. That would allow me to buy enough gas to drive back to GLBI. At the time, gas cost $.20-.25 per gallon.

    I checked the mileage on the trip to Wisconsin, and noted that I was getting 15-

16 MPG. I drove around White Lake some, then to Gerald's home, and his bride's home. After singing at the wedding, I tried to find Gerald to get the money he had promised, so that I could refill the gas tank and drive home. He was nowhere to be found – in his excitement to go on his honeymoon, he had already left.

I had a couple of dollars, so I pumped that much gas into the car's tank, knowing it would not be enough to get us back. I started home with my wife, our baby, Kathy, and my wife's brother, Gary, with no idea of what I would do. I kept this from my wife, as I didn't want to worry her.

I watched the gas gauge, and it seemed to go down faster than ever. We reached Fon du Lac, WI, and the gauge showed "empty". I pulled over to the side of the road, and tears came to my eyes as I told my wife, "We're on empty, what can we do?".

I suggested that we call a local pastor and borrow some money for gas to get home. Looking at the map, I realized that we were still about 120 miles from home. I had 87 cents in change – that was all we had. I knew that even if I could use that for gas, it wouldn't get us home, and we might be stranded somewhere in a dark, remote area away from any town. I was in a desperate situation and didn't know what to do.

Wanda spoke up, "We have told others to believe God for anything, so we need to believe God to get us home. Let's lay our hands on the dashboard and pray that God will stretch the gas for us. We know He answers prayer." <u>What a wife!!</u> We prayed as she suggested, that God would stretch the gas like he did the cruse of oil for the widow in Elijah's day.

This was serious business. I pulled the car back onto the highway and started for home, 120 miles away. Every time I looked at the gas gauge, it read "empty". On and on we drove. Finally, as we approached Zion, IL, we began to thank God. With a final word of praise, we pulled up to our home. <u>I still had the 87 cents.</u>

The next day, Guy Stambaugh and I calculated the gas mileage I had gotten on the trip back to Zion – 35 MPG in this big, heavy car that had never before gotten more than 15-16 MPG. The days of miracles are not past. We just have to exercise faith to believe.

8. In May, 1975, I accepted the pastorate of North Mesquite Assembly of God church. It was a small congregation of 50-60 people. It began to grow, and the folks in the neighborhood recognized that something was happening at the church. A family who had previously attended the Methodist church next door began to attend our church.

The Englands, in their late 70's, cared for their son Kenneth, who had MS, and his wife, who had crippling arthritis. Both got around in wheelchairs, even at home. Kenneth was in worse physical shape than his wife. She could walk some, though very awkwardly.

Kenneth, his wife, and his parents were always in the Sunday morning services and occasionally in the Sunday evening services. Kenneth was always in his wheelchair. One particular Sunday morning, God was moving in a powerful way. People were rejoicing, and the glorious presence of God filled the building.

Kenneth wheeled his chair to the front and said, "I want to be healed, get out of this chair, and walk." I anointed Kenneth's forehead with oil, and several of us gathered around him to pray that God would raise him up and enable him to walk again. Taking Kenneth by the hand, I instructed him to get to his feet in the name of Jesus Christ and for his glory.

Kenneth struggled to his feet, steadied himself for a minute or two, then took three or four steps, smiling and praising God. He proceeded to walk to the back of the church, pushing his wheelchair. By this time, "holy bedlam" was taking place as people shouted, laughed with joy, and danced in the Spirit. Many were weeping.

That Sunday morning, Kenneth pushed his wheelchair to the vestibule, out the door, and across the parking lot to the family car. The church began to grow from that time on, and became the fastest-growing A/G church in all of North Texas.

9. I had been asked by Bill Fox, a hunting and fishing buddy from Bible school days, to

come and preach for his church on a weekend. He was now pastoring a Baptist church in Ava, IL. Bill and Glory Fox had just re-connected with my wife and I after our paths had taken us in different directions. We planned to spend a day or two with them.

As we started out from our home, rain began to sprinkle us. We gave it little thought and took off, hoping it wasn't going to rain the whole time we were gone. As we traveled, the rain began to come down heavier. Many of the state highways are blacktop, and oil from vehicles combined with a little rain can make the surface quite slick.

I slowed down somewhat, but coming up over a railroad overpass at Flora, IL, our car began to slide. I lost control of the car, and my wife screamed out as we jumped the curb, barely missing the barrier that was designed to keep cars from falling to the railroad tracks below.

The Oldsmobile 88 I was driving had a hood ornament in the shape of a rocket. As we jumped the curb and headed down the embankment, covered in long, wet rye grass, I saw a telephone pole directly in our path. The pole was centered on the rocket hood ornament. A strange thought came to my mind – "We're going to hit that pole right where that rocket is pointing."

There was no way to avoid the telephone pole. The embankment was steep, the grass was slick with rain, and the car was heavy. I felt there was nothing I could do. I just prayed, "Lord Jesus, help us."

The next thing I remembered was the car hitting a small ditch at the bottom of the embankment. I sat there numb for a minute, then made sure my family was not injured. Everyone seemed to be fine, except for being a bit shaken up. I wondered for a moment how we missed the telephone pole. There was no humanly-possible way to avoid slamming into it.

Suddenly, a police cruiser pulled up, the officer got out and walked down to where we sat. He asked how we were and what had happened. I explained to him that I had lost control on the slick pavement and had been unable to correct my slide.

With a stub of a cigar in the corner of his mouth, he pushed back his military-style cap on his head, and with tears in his eyes, said, "Preacher, there was someone else in that front seat besides you, your wife, and your baby. Look up that hill. Your tire tracks were heading directly toward that telephone pole." There's no way you could have turned that car up and around that pole on the long, wet grass."

I looked back up the hill and could see our tracks centering on the pole, then just a few feet from it, the tracks curving <u>uphill</u>. "That is humanly impossible", said the officer, with a quiver in his voice. "The Good Lord was with you – that is a miracle." I had to agree with him, and I said, "Praise the Lord."

No one was hurt, and the only damage was a broken front axle on the driver's side. I remembered that we had asked for God's protection on us before we left home, as we usually did. <u>He cares</u>.

10. It was raining that night as I started home from my job at Sears, Roebuck in Alton, IL. My wife had headed home in her car to Grafton, IL, a small river town at the confluence of the Illinois and Mississippi

rivers. I had to close the register and wait for a young man to whom I was giving a ride home. He lived on my way home at the Clifton Terrace area along the Great River Road.

This road was eventually to extend from the headwaters of the Mississippi all the way to the Gulf of Mexico. There were no lights along the road, and it was as dark as pitch. The rain made it even worse. We were talking and not really paying attention to the road, because few people were out in that weather.

Suddenly, he yelled, "Look out, there's a lady you're about to hit!" There, standing by the rear of a car, was a woman. Her car was angled so her lights were shining down into a ravine off to my right. Her taillights were almost invisible because of the angle they were pointing.

I swerved, but I was too late. She had seen me coming and had jumped around to the side of her car. I hit the rear end of her car and knocked her down. Another car carrying a man and wife had stopped in the median between the four lanes of the highway. I bounced off the first car and hit the other one almost head-on.

The young man riding with me said he heard me say, "Jesus, this is it." That's all I said. I really thought I was going to die that night on that road. I sat in the car, too stunned to speak. I'm sure many would know how weak I felt.

Others stopped and pried open the doors of my car. They asked how we were. I had a small cut, actually more of a scratch, and the young man with me had a knot on his head where his head had struck the windshield. About this time, a state trooper arrived and began to process what had happened.

The woman who had stopped on the highway and left her car at such an angle had done so because another car carrying a man and woman had gone off the road into the ravine, on the right side of the road. She had parked her car at that angle to shine her headlights down into the ravine, preventing me from seeing her taillights.

She was not injured, but the couple in the median, whose car I had hit head on, had to be transported to the hospital by ambulance. The couple whose car had gone off the highway into the ravine were fine, just shook up. The trooper got the wreckage onto the shoulder, then asked me to go with him to the hospital to check on the couple who were injured and give my statement.

As we were standing at the hospital, I suddenly began to black out. I had been under quite a bit of stress, and my adrenaline had kept me going, but now shock was setting in. Some of the hospital staffers caught me, laid me on a gurney, and covered me with a blanket.

The couple in the median were more seriously hurt. One of the man's legs was broken in a couple of places, and he had a punctured lung. The woman had some rather bad cuts. They were alive, for which I thanked God.

My car could not be towed. It was so mangled that it had to be cut into two sections, right behind the front doors. People were amazed that we walked away with no more than a scratch. However, I know that when I uttered the name of Jesus, He took over.

He's still in charge.

11. The highway stretched out in front of me like a shining ribbon. We were traveling west and the sun was high in the sky. We were driving to visit my wife's uncle Bus in El Centro, CA. Our plans were also to visit her brother in Yucaipa, CA, and spend some time with them.

I had been following a bread truck for what seemed like an eternity. The two-lane highway was wide, but whenever I got ready to pass, another car would approach from the other direction. A number of times, I pulled out and then ducked back in behind the bread truck.

Again I pulled out, and the road seemed to be clear. The driver of the bread truck, who sat up much higher, and could (I thought) see more clearly than I, motioned for me to come around him. I started out, and got just about even with his front end, when I saw an 18-wheeler in the left lane. There was no way I could drop back, and I was too close to the bread truck to cut in.

I was afraid that if I went to the left shoulder, the 18-wheeler would go there also, and we would collide. I really don't know what happened next. I heard my wife scream, and the next thing I knew, we were sitting on the shoulder of the highway on the opposite side of the road.

I don't know how I missed the bread truck, the 18-wheeler, or the ditch. All I knew is that the car was fine, nobody was hurt, and I was as weak as a kitten. We sat here for a few minutes, thanking God that our guardian angel took over. Either that car had wings, or God lifted it out of the way of danger.

I know it was God taking care of us.

12. My wife and I had been to a bed and breakfast in East Texas and were returning home to Mesquite, TX. It was a nasty night. The storm was causing the visibility to be almost zero. The rain was coming down in buckets, as it can in Texas during a storm.

I thought I was being careful. We were within the city limits of Mesquite, about five miles from home. There were places on the highway on which the car would almost hydroplane due to the pooling of water. Suddenly, I hit one of those spots on the rain-slick blacktop. I started to slide.

Normally, I would turn into the slide to gain control, but as I hydroplaned, the Lincoln turned end-to-end, and I was traveling backward. The car went down through the median, up on the other side of the highway. I kept trying to gain control of the car, but I could not.

I looked in my rear-view mirror, and I was startled to see an oncoming tractor-trailer, in the same lane in which I was traveling backward. Suddenly, something or someone took the steering wheel out of my hands, steered the car down into the median, and spun us back in the right direction, headed out of danger.

I drove on to the church I pastored, so weak I thought I would collapse. When we parked, I saw I had lost a hubcap and part of my tailpipe. There was grass and mud caught in the bumper and underneath the car, but no damage to the body of the car.

I know that the "Someone" who took over the steering wheel is the same "Someone" who has promised to take care of His children - my precious Lord, Jesus Christ.

13. I looked through the window of the nursery at Alton Memorial Hospital in Alton, IL. What I saw was a beautiful baby boy, my second son, Kent, who was as orange as a pumpkin. I began to cry. The doctor, Edwin Buzan, had told my wife and me just a few hours earlier that our child's liver was not functioning properly, and unless things changed he would either die, be mentally retarded, or be in a vegetative state.

Both of us had looked forward so to this child, and now we were told he might not live. I left the hospital that night with a heavy heart. As I drove home to Granite City, IL, I could hardly see for the tears. I prayed out loud to God. My heart was heavy, yet I knew that God had all things in His control.

The doctors planned to do a complete blood change, to try to cause the child's liver to begin functioning properly. If it was successful, the bilirubin count, which was very high, would begin to go down, and our baby would be OK.

The next day, I went to the hospital and my wife told me that the bilirubin count had gone down as a result of the blood change. We were elated, and thanked the Lord for what we knew was answered prayer. We thought we would be able to take our baby home within a day or two.

However, that was not to be. Dr Buzan came into the room, and I knew by the look on his face that something was wrong. He said, "The count is going up again, and it has reached dangerous levels." I felt as if the bottom had dropped out of my world. "Why, God? Hadn't I prayed, and hadn't I been a faithful servant? Why?"

Wanda began to cry, and so did I. I said, "Doc, isn't there anything you can do? There must be something." He replied, "We're going to do another blood change, and maybe this second one will correct the problem." We agreed, and as he left, we began to cry and pray.

That night, I had planned to stay awake until the blood change was completed. After the blood change, a nurse came to tell us that the count was going down again. I was so relieved – now, maybe, this crisis was over. I stopped by the window of the nursery, put my hand on the glass in the baby's direction, and prayed, "Lord, keep it going down." I left and made the long, lonely drive home.

The next day I called the nurse's station and was told that the count had continued to go down and would soon be normal. However, I received a call later in the day from Dr. Buzan. It was not good news – the count had begun to rise again. The blood change seemed not to be working.

I asked him if my wife knew, and he said that she had been told. I knew I needed to get to the hospital as quickly as possible. Honestly, my faith at that point was very low. But whatever was to happen, my wife and I would face it together.

I expected her to be a "basket case" by the time I arrived. I hated that drive more than any other I remember. My son's life hung in the balance. My precious wife, who had carried this child for nine months, was grieving her heart out right then, I knew.

As I approached her room, I tried to put a calm look on my face. I opened the door, and as I walked in, she was smiling. I couldn't believe my eyes. She said, "Honey, God gave me a scripture from His Word. Let me read it to you. It's from Psalm 57." As she read verses 1 and 2, my heart leaped within my chest. No matter what was to happen, He had let her know, and now me, that He had not forsaken or forgotten us. It would be all right.

The bilirubin count continued to climb, even above what they deemed the highest level possible without damage. At midnight, Dr. Buzan came into my wife's room. His face and demeanor showed the strain of having to share with us the bad news.

We told him the situation was in God's hands, and that we were at peace with that. We asked if he would pray with us before he left, and he agreed. He and I knelt beside my wife's bed, and we all agreed that whatever happened now was in the hands of God. As he left the room, Dr. Buzan said, "It's in the hands of a higher power now."

I left the hospital that night deeply concerned, but with a peace in my heart. It was a restless night for me. Early the next morning, I called the hospital to ask how the count was going. The nurse reported that it had started to go down during the night, and that it had kept going down, to the point that everything seemed to be functioning as it should.

When I arrived at the hospital, I looked in the nursery window, and I could tell that our child looked less "orange-colored". Later that day we were told that everything was now normal and he was "out of the woods". A few days later we took home our "miracle child".

This was truly the most precious miracle I experienced, because it involved my own flesh and blood. Today, Kent is "as strong as a bull" physically, and his IQ is, I'm sure, higher than my own. He is a strong man spiritually, as well. (*Note from Kent: I have an MS in Journalism, and have bench-pressed more than 470# - glory to God!*)

I will never forget the hours when his life hung in the balance, and many times, when

I look at him, the words "He is a miracle from God" cross my mind.

14. I was asked to preach a funeral for one of the members of a church I had previously pastored in Bridgeport, IL. I mentioned this to the Board of Deacons at the church I then pastored in Sherman, TX.

Everett Mitchell, one of the Deacons, had his own airplane, which he used in his construction business. He offered to fly me to Illinois and back, since he had a business commitment nearby in Indiana. He said he would fly me to the airport just outside of Lawrenceville, IL, continue on to his destination, and then pick me up on his way home to Texas. The trip wouldn't cost me anything, since he had to travel that direction on business anyway.

The flight to Illinois was a joy. The weather was beautiful, and the four-seater plane performed perfectly. In seemingly no time, my daughter, Kathy, and I had arrived at our destination. I said goodbye to Everett and Lamar Waller, who worked for him, and told them we would see them later that day after the funeral.

After the funeral we were driven back to the airport by some friends. Everett was already on the ground refueling and checking out the plane. Kathy and I got aboard. I sat in the seat next to the pilot. Kathy sat behind the pilot next to Mr. Waller. Soon, we were airborne and headed home.

We anticipated that we would get home around 7:30 that evening. We crossed over into Missouri airspace and saw, ahead of us, a tremendous storm. Everett tried to contact the FAA about the direction and strength of the storm, but he couldn't get through. Finally a response came, but just as suddenly, Everett said, "We're in the storm."

The plane began to be battered by the storm, suddenly dropping 500 to 1,000 feet and taking our breath away. It was hard to even see the nose of the plane through the windshield. The plane would suddenly rise, and just as suddenly dip right or left. Rain and hail rattled the walls and roof.

I could tell we were in updrafts and downdrafts. It was difficult to know if we were right side up or upside down. The look on Everett's face let me know we were in a perilous situation.

I was frightened and felt as if I would be sick. Mr. Waller was feeling it too. But when I looked at Kathy, she was fast asleep. Silently, I started to pray – hard.

The plane was bouncing around so much that it was all Everett could do to keep it from breaking apart. I knew it was going to be tough to get through this. The pilot said that if we could find a hole through the clouds and storm, we could descend to a lower, safer level.

We had to be careful that we didn't slam into one of the Ozark mountains. Mr. Mitchell said to pray for a hole in the clouds, so I did. In just a few minutes, I spotted a small hole off to our right, and we dove through it. Amazingly, we found that we were right above the Little Rock, Arkansas airport.

We received clearance and landed. We all let out a sigh of relief and said, "Thank you, Lord." After that harrowing experience, we all decided to get rooms in a local motel, get a meal, and have a good night's sleep before venturing on the next morning.

The next day was glorious, and we flew home without incident. I asked Kathy, "How could you sleep through all that?", and she said, "Dad, it wouldn't have done any good to worry, it was all in God's hands anyway". And, you know, she was right.

I was almost ashamed to say that I had been scared. What a gal!

15. When I drove up to the church I pastored in Bridgeport, IL, I noticed that the door to the evangelist quarters was open. I began to chide myself for forgetting to lock that door when I left the night before. However, on closer inspection, I saw marks on the door facing that showed the door to have been "jimmied". It looked as if a screwdriver or a pry bar had been used to open the door.

I went around to the front and looked, and the front door was still locked. I then went back through the door that had been forced open and entered the kitchen area. I noticed that a radio we kept there was gone. I then went into the bedroom and looked around. I pushed open the door to the adjoining bathroom, and everything in there looked fine.

I went home to tell my wife about the incident and call the local police, and also the county sheriff, who was a friend of mine. I met them back at the church a few minutes later. We looked around the church and discovered a bank that sat on the communion table had been broken into and that some things were missing from the Sunday School office.

The Sheriff informed me that there had also been a break-in at the local hardware and lumber store. The thief (or thieves) had taken money, a .32 caliber pistol, and some other items. The Sheriff suspected that a local man who was wanted for some other break-ins in the nearby town of Olney was responsible. He was a big man, 250 pounds, 6'1" tall, who was often involved in unlawful activities and had a long "rap sheet".

After the police left, I had one of our men add a deadbolt lock to the outside door of the evangelist quarters. An inventory of the missing items showed that their total value was far less than $100, so we made no claim to our insurance company.

A few days later I received a call from the Sheriff. He said that he had our radio and some other items here, and we would like you to come over to Lawrenceville (the location of the county seat and the county jail) to identify them. I went that afternoon, and indeed those items were the ones taken from our evangelist quarters.

The sheriff mentioned that he had in custody the man who had stolen the items from our church and from the hardware store, and that the prisoner wanted to speak with me. The sheriff had me wait in an interview room, and in a few minutes he ushered in this scruffy individual he had previously described to me. The sheriff left us alone, but said he would be nearby.

I asked the man his name and why he had broken into a church. He said that he was desperate and needed a place to hide. But his next statement sent cold chills up and down my spine. He said, "Preacher, when you opened the door to the bathroom, I was behind that door with the .32 pistol in my hand - if you had stepped inside that bathroom, I would have shot you."

I hadn't walked into the bathroom, but only opened the door and looked into the shower, just inside the door. He was less than 3 feet away from me and I hadn't known it. When I went to my home to call the Sheriff, he slipped out.

He asked me to forgive him, and I did. I tried to talk to him about the Lord, but he said he wasn't ready for that. He did, however, ask if I would pray for him. I sensed that he "didn't have all his oars in the water".

I walked out of the county jail that day and my legs were like jelly. But I thanked God for his protection. I found out later that the man had indeed been armed, but had forgotten to steal any ammunition for the gun. I think it was a miracle of God's protection.

16.   I was excited to be going to Russia. The Iron Curtain had fallen some time before, and people, even preachers, were being allowed in. The group I was to travel with was taking in plain Bibles, study Bibles, and gospel tracts, all printed in Russian. The group was made up of lay people and ministers.

We were from different parts of the United States, and we were to meet at Finnish Airlines in New York City. Our airline schedule allowed us about an hour and 15 minutes to go from our landing gate to where we were to meet our traveling party.

We embarked on American Airlines from Dallas-Fort Worth airport and traveled to St. Louis, where we changed planes. From St. Louis, we were to fly on TWA to New York. Our flight took off about 15 minutes late from D/FW airport, but our pilot told us that we had a tailwind and would make up some of the time – for which we were grateful.

The flight to St. Louis was relaxing, and we arrived at close to the appointed time. We hurried over to the TWA gate in plenty of time to board. We pulled away from the gate and suddenly our plane stopped. The pilot's voice came over the intercom and told us the plane had to return to the gate to have something checked.

We were told that we would be airborne in 15 minutes. Those 15 minutes passed, then 25 minutes. The pilot then informed us that we would be taking off after 15 more minutes. After 50 minutes, we finally took off.

I was so upset as we sat on the tarmac, because I knew that we were running late. The pilot told us that he could make up some time, but this turned out not to be true.

When we arrived at the New York airport we had five minutes to get from our gate to the Finnish Airlines terminal. We were told that it was a long distance from where we were. We began to run, trying to drag all our luggage behind us.

Our luggage was falling off the two-wheeled carts we were using, and we were bumping into other passengers. We arrived, panting and sweating, at the ticket counter for Finnish Airlines. We showed our tickets to the airline employee and were told that we were too late. The plane had already pulled away from the gate and was heading toward the runway for takeoff.

I said, "Ma'am, we have to be on that flight. We don't know where the rest of our party will be staying in St. Petersburg, Russia. All we know is that they are staying at a St Petersburg hotel, but we have no idea which one."

She very firmly and angrily said, "You will have to wait until tomorrow." We replied that we could not do that, because we had nowhere to stay in New York City – we had to get on that flight. She became even more upset, and said that we would have to wait until tomorrow, and TWA would pay for our hotel stay.

I knew this was impossible, so I turned to my friend Jim Guess, and said, "Jim, let's pray. We need a miracle." We turned away from the counter, and I prayed a very simple prayer. It mostly consisted of "God, help!".

As we were praying, another representative of Finnish Airlines came running up the tunnel toward us. She yelled, "Do those men need to get on that plane?". The lady at the counter replied, "Yes, but I told them it was too late." The employee who had just arrived said, "No, the plane has returned to the terminal for some reason, and they can board!".

We shouted, "Praise the Lord!", and ran, with our luggage, out to the plane. They explained that our luggage would be loading, and we got on the plane. The rest of our traveling party were already on the plane, and they were elated that we had made it. I asked if they knew why the plane had returned to the terminal, but no one had heard a thing about it.

I asked a stewardess, but she didn't know, either. No one knew the reason the plane had returned, but I did. The Lord heard our prayer, and, once more, changed the course of events. Everyone exclaimed, "A miracle!".

And now, as Paul Harvey says, "The Rest of the Story". Because of our last-minute boarding, our checked baggage had not arrived with us. All we had were our carry-on bags. We were upset, but the airline promised that our bags would arrive the next day. Sure enough, we received a call the next day that our luggage was at the airport.

The next day, Jim and I, with our InTourist guide (an employee of the Russian government) took a taxi to the airport. God spoke to my heart and told me "Instead of being angry about the lost luggage, use this opportunity to minister – witness to your guide about salvation".

The 45-minute drive to the airport ended up providing an opportunity to lead our guide to the Lord outside the Customs office. She prayed the "Sinner's Prayer" and we promised her one of the Bibles from our suitcases as soon as we retrieved them. I knew then why the plan was late in New York, why the Finnish Air plane returned to the gate, and why my luggage was late – all because God had an appointment with a Russian InTourist guide.

17. We had traveled from St. Petersburg, Russia, to Moscow. On a Thursday evening, we were to speak and be part of a prayer meeting in a hotel on the outskirts of Moscow. We arrived at our hotel and found 110-120 people, mostly between the ages of 17 and 35. We had a great worship time and a number of youth testified. I spoke for a few minutes through an interpreter, although many of those in attendance understood English.

At the close of the service there were a number of people who came forward for prayer. Some accepted Christ as their Savior, and some came to pray with us about other spiritual or physical needs.

Most of the young people in attendance were praising and glorifying the Lord.

There were also clusters of people praying further back in the crowd - most of the chairs had been moved aside to make room. From one of the prayer groups further back, someone came over to my group, saying that I was needed in the other group. After following this person back to the other cluster of individuals, I saw a young man writhing on the floor.

He was making strange, guttural sounds and was foaming at the mouth. We immediately realized that he was possessed by one or more demons. We all gathered around him, laid our hands on him, and began rebuking the demon spirits in the power of Jesus' name.

We interceded for 20-30 minutes, then, suddenly, a glow came over his face. The strange sounds ceased, his entire demeanor changed, and he expressed his joy at being free. Soon after this, we returned to our hotel room.

The following Sunday afternoon, we attended a youth rally at a former Communist opera house. The Hammer and

Sickle insignia was still on the side walls of the building alongside the Red Star. We had a glorious service, after which at least 70 people accepted Christ.

As I was leaving the service with our group, a young man standing to one side spoke to me in Russian. Our guide interpreted what the man was saying.

This was the same young man who had been set free from demon possession on the previous Thursday evening. He didn't even appear to be the same person, but he told me he was free and was now following Christ.

18. I had taken my first full-time pastorate at the age of 23. I was excited at the opportunity to pastor full-time without having to work a secular job on the side. My first son, Kevin, had just been born a few months earlier, and my wife and daughter had settled into life at the parsonage.

We immediately began seeing God work in very special ways. People began to be excited about what God was doing. Many were getting right with God; we saw new faces every week, and the church was growing in many ways.

One of the members owned an Archways cookie franchise, catering to stores in the Eastern and Southern parts of Illinois. He and his wife had one child, a boy of about 11, whose name was Ronnie.

Ronnie was plagued with very serious nosebleeds. There were so bad that they could not be stopped by normal methods, and he would usually end up in the Robinson, IL hospital. When the nosebleeds started, they left him weak, and he had become very anemic.

One Sunday morning in church, Ronnie's nose began to bleed. His father and mother tried to stop the bleeding, and friends offered suggestions, but nothing worked – the bleeding continued unabated. At the beginning of the morning Worship Service, Ronnie's parents brought him to the front of the church for special prayer.

As I prepared to pray for Ronnie, God spoke to me, saying, "I want you to anoint him with oil, then put both your little fingers in his nostrils." I didn't question God about this unorthodox procedure; I simply did it. I'm sure those looking on thought I had gone crazy. I prayed, removed my fingers from his nostrils, and the bleeding stopped immediately.

I pastored there for another year, and Ronnie never had another nosebleed.

19.   We had flown into Lucknow, India from New Delhi, and met missionaries Robert and Helen Sullivan, who were working in that area. A few evenings after ministering to students in a Bible school, my wife and I were asked to go with the missionaries to a remote village about 25 kilometers from Lucknow. This village had only recently been ministered to by a native preacher.

We traveled over treacherous dirt roads that were partially washed out, with drops of 8-10 feet. I held my breath many times, imagining what it would be like coming back along that road in the dark.

Finally, the car came to a stop and we walked the ¼ mile off the road to the village. The village was made up of clay bricks plastered with cow dung. The thatched roofs kept what little rain the village got out of the huts. Around 300 people lived here.

We began to sing and praise the Lord. Soon, most of the village was gathered in front of the little porch of the hut near which we were standing. After a few minutes, I began to preach through an interpreter. Then something strange happened.

A young man of 15 or 16 began to writhe on the ground like a serpent and emit growling sounds. The crowd was disturbed, but we recognized that the young man was possessed by a demon. I stopped preaching and the missionaries and I grabbed the young man and rebuked the demon, telling him to come out in Jesus' name.

Almost immediately he ceased his writhing, and within a few moments was sitting on the ground smiling. We shared with the villagers that the God we served is all-powerful, and had delivered this young man from demon spirits. I then invited the crowd to make Jesus Christ the one they worshipped and served.

After seeing what happened to the young man and hearing these words, most of the village responded by raising their hands to indicate that they wanted to receive Christ. I led them in the sinners' prayer. The head man of the village, who had been drunk, sobered up and told us he was giving the choicest lot, near the road, to hold a church building for the village. Indeed, a church was erected there soon after we returned stateside.

20.   My wife and I were headed out on some errands. It was a cool, blustery day. We had traveled just ¼ mile from our home when we saw a lady walking with two bags of groceries. She was laboring heavily under her load, and was not wearing enough clothing to stay warm. She was nicely dressed, but the clothes weren't appropriate for that weather. Neither were her high-heeled shoes, which only added to her difficulties.
I pulled over to the side of the road and asked if we could give her a lift. My wife quickly explained that I was a pastor nearby, at North Mesquite Assembly of God.

She hesitated for a bit, then accepted our offer. As she entered our car, she explained that her car had broken down and she was walking home.

I remarked to here that it looked as if she was really struggling with her load, and asked her where she lived. She replied that she lived in some apartments off Chaha Road, which quite surprised me. Chaha Road was five miles from where we were. I told her, "Dear lady, there is no way you could have made it that far with your load."

She was an attractive young lady, and she smiled and asked if it would be a problem for us to take her so far. I explained that the Lord had caused us to stop and help her, and she was grateful.

There was not much talk as we headed out Interstate 30 toward the Chaha Road exit. She told us where to turn in for her apartments, since there were so many complexes in that area. We pulled into the complex she indicated, and I offered to take her as close as possible to her apartment. She declined, saying that was not necessary.

I stopped the car, and she got out. My wife said, "Maybe you should help her with her load." I stepped out of the car to help her, but there was no one there. There was no way she could have walked or even ran to the apartments, which were 50-60 feet from the car.

I looked around, and there was no young lady; there were no groceries. Dumbfounded, I turned to my wife and said, "Did you see where she went?". With a puzzled look on her face, she replied, "This is weird." I opened the back door to look at the seat on which she'd been sitting, and there was a $20 bill there.

I looked around our car again, and there was no one visible anywhere around. I slid back in the driver's seat, trembling. I said, "Wanda, we have just attended an angel, who knew we needed $20. There was no other possible explanation.

...Light the Corners of my Mind

My poor wife is sick of reading about herself, and my sensitive, thoughtful response to her feelings is: "Too stinkin' bad!". As I write this, I'm away from my sweetie for another series of days – several states away, in fact. On the way back from my client to my hotel, I heard a song that reminded me of a standout memory we made early in our relationship, and that triggered others...

1. Slow-dancing with her at her daughter's wedding reception, although "dancing" is an exaggeration. We hugged while I shuffled my feet and gazed into the face of this lady who so captured my heart.

2. The first time I saw her in person, as she came through the door for our first date. She smiled at me, and the air around her face lit up.

3. A text she sent me in which she called me a "sweet man". For some reason, this confirmed to me that someone could indeed see something loveable in me, though I had

become convinced that I was barely tolerable.

4. Poking around the deserted farmhouse we eventually bought, and describing to her how I wanted to make a life with her there.

5. Realizing that the dreams she shared with me when we were dating have now come true, and that we get to come up with new ones.

6. Seeing her for the first time in work clothes, as I joined her to help her grandfather move from the 100-acre farm he had gotten too old to work. I was amazed at how cute this lady was in work boots and a ball cap.

7. First kiss – Oh, my... Nothing rude or crude – just a kiss, on our 3rd date, but... Oh, my!

8. The first time we prayed together about something. I believe we were considering the purchase of the farmhouse property where we now live. I discovered that this lady knew how to pray! Thinking more about it now, I shouldn't have been surprised that a single mom with a teenager knew how to pray effectively. Just the fact that the teen boy was still alive was proof of that!

9. Interpreting for her with a Spanish-speaking client when she was working Hospice. I was a Volunteer, and it was... interesting to see the curious looks we got when the Latina spoke English and the Gringo translated!

10. Yesterday. I love this lady more deeply, just before our 5th Valentine's Day together, than I knew I could love a person. She just keeps getting better, wiser, more beautiful, and more capable. So, happy VD, baby! (Wait - that doesn't sound right...)

And my heart goes, "Boom, Boom, Boom"...

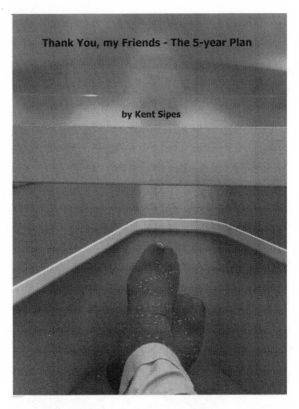

Cover photo from the 1ˢᵗ book – my feet up in a 1ˢᵗ-class berth. My sweetie is not responsible for the hole in my sock.

Dance, Sing, Snore, Scream

Really, I *tried* to be cultured. I'm not one of those folks who just hates "uppity" things like opera and ballet – I've actually been to one of each. I've even tried to appreciate modern art (with no luck). And I actually used to listen to Classical music <u>voluntarily</u>.

Both of my regular readers may remember my "list of things I'll never do again" (*A 6 for A 9*), and recall that attending an opera is on the list of things someone would have to <u>pay</u> me to do again. My opera experience was as positive as it could have been (unless power chords had been involved) – I attended with my wife, free, in really good seats. She was spending the weekend with me in Chicago, where I was working for a local college district.

I had met the Music Director for the Chicago Lyric Opera on a flight, and he had offered two free tickets to enhance whatever weekend my wife came to play tourist. We saw *Don Giovanni* (in Italian, of course), featuring a plot of sin, deceit, and eventual condemnation to Hell – Ooh, what cheery entertainment, right? All singing, no dialogue

Well, I set my mind to try and enjoy this new experience – I wanted to give it a fair chance. I studied the program to try and understand the story; I read profiles of the main singers, and I made sure I knew where to look for the English subtitles. Finally, the house lights dimmed, the orchestra began to play, and the lead character appeared on the stage and began to sing about how he had fulfilled his lusts in the past, and how he planned to continue doing so.

And then he repeated himself. And then he told his life story, in several more verses. His butler appeared, and he repeated to the butler his plans for satiating his desires, and which woman was to be his latest conquest. The butler joined him in the song, bemoaning the fact that he was forced to help facilitate such evil plans, then Don Giovanni ordered him to go make everything ready for the evening's activities.

... And then his intended victim came onstage and sang about her maiden virtue for several minutes, and how sad she was that she had no option but to spend the evening with this powerful man, though he had an evil reputation. And then she sang about how she dreaded it... for about 10 minutes...and I began to relate to her dread.

I looked at the time on my phone, and there were still 2 hours of the performance to go, plus intermission. That was when I realized why wine is sold in the lobby during intermission, and wondered why <u>stronger</u> painkillers are not available.

Again, I told myself to try and enjoy the wonderful voices, the power and the range of these world-class singers. I marveled at the high-dollar special effects created for the performance, and the wonderful acoustics of the auditorium. And that ate up another 5 minutes – only an hour and 45 minutes to go!

Finally, it was time for intermission. We went to the lobby to stretch our legs, and grab snacks and drinks, and I looked for something solid against which to bang my head, to give me something else on which to concentrate besides the tedium. Too quickly, intermission was over, and the Opera recommenced. Only an hour to go – keep hope alive!

Interminable singing followed, as Don Giovanni seduced the poor girl, after which she went on and on about her shame and regret. Then Don began to make plans for further conquests, at which time the devil showed up and dragged him to Hell. Never before have I <u>cheered</u> the devil, but I was so happy that he removed the main character, because that meant the ordeal was over.

As the house lights came back up, I tried not to show how tedious I found the performance, in case my wife had really liked it. But when I asked her how she enjoyed it, her response was akin to that of a young man from Bulgaria who attended a Christian Rock concert with our church back in the 1980s – when asked about what he thought of the concert afterward, he very seriously said, "It was... an experience..."

Why, yes – attending an opera was a once-in-a-lifetime... experience. Been there, done that, and they don't sell t-shirts (or nachos). Now, ask me about my experience with *The Nutcracker* ballet...

Redemption Cookies

I bake cookies – not with much ambition, since I typically use either a cookie mix or refrigerated break-off dough*, then add "extras" (like dark chocolate chips and/or pecans), before baking. A few years ago, I was asked to bake cookies for a bake sale to benefit our Kids' Ministry, so I baked 24 large chocolate-chip cookies, packaged and priced them as directed, and put them out for display with the other baked goods for sale in our church foyer.

Soon, other church members began to arrive, including a precocious 6-year-old girl named Hazel. When I was very new to our church, and knew hardly anyone, this amazing tyke had stuck out her hand and introduced herself as if she were at least 10 years older. This so impressed me that I began watching for her to show up at church, so that I could say "Hi!" to someone whose name I knew (and how could I forget?).

I immediately squatted down to her eye level and asked, "Hazel, don't you need a cookie?" – to which she replied, "Why no, I don't believe I do... I've just had breakfast..." Uh, no. I've never before heard that answer from a munchkin. Of course she needed a cookie!

So, after clearing it with her grandmother, we made our way out to the bake sale table, where Hazel proceeded to pick out a bag of my cookies as exactly what she wanted. So I paid for the cookies, gave her the baggie, and she was a happy kid.

Only later that day did I grasp the irony of what had happened. I had purchased the ingredients, assembled them, baked the cookies, then packaged them and given them away. I then bought back my own cookies for the benefit of someone else, who consumed them (with gusto!). Yep, I redeemed those cookies.

And that's when I finally understood the meaning of the word: redemption. God created everything from nothing, assembled it beautifully, then gave it to us (with simple instructions!). We ignored His instructions, and sold ourselves into slavery. God took pity on us and bought back our rights & privileges by sending Jesus as payment for our rebellion.

My cookies made Hazel happy for a few minutes. Maybe she also got the idea that another grownup not related to her thought she was important. But the redemption that *God* did was vastly more important, because with that action, God said that Hazel (and I) are important. And, as I figured out many years ago, if God says you're important – you are!

He wanted real life for us, and wanted to give us the chance to be with Him forever, so much that Jesus became separated from God, first by entering time and coming to Earth, then by taking our ugly, warped nature into Himself. God can't be around imperfection, so Jesus was split from the Father for the first time ever! Then Jesus died, as the penalty for *our* sinful choices.

So, don't *you* need a cookie?

When we were just courting – that face!!

Worlds Away – pt. 1

Traffic was more than daunting in Mumbai, India – it was bumper-to-bumper, with as many lanes traveling one way as cars that could fit on the pavement, uniformly traveling at 20 MPH. The use of turn signals prior to changing lanes was an invitation to be cut off before a car could enter the tiny space between vehicles into which its driver intended to press it.

Pedestrians do not have the right-of-way, and there are no designated crosswalks. Catching the eye of a driver to request that he/she stop for a moment so that I could cross into my next potentially-deadly encounter was a chancy matter. While Indian drivers are very friendly to visitors, they are also in a <u>great</u> hurry. Striking me with their vehicle would be harmful to a driver's karma, but it would also get me out of his way (and there would probably be an opportunity to fix the karma later).

This was my first foray outside the hotel since I had arrived at the airport and been picked up by my assigned driver, who spoke very little English, but was enthusiastically dedicated to preserving my life and helping me get around Mumbai. Apparently, this was a really good gig for him. I checked into my room, unpacked my suitcase, and lay down on the bed for a nap (beginning at 3 AM). At 10 AM, I woke with the desire to "experience India".

I showered, dressed, and traveled down to the lobby to inquire at the front desk as to what there was to see within walking distance. The hotel staffer with whom I spoke was concerned that I was considering venturing out on my own, but assured me that I was probably safe, as long as I stayed in public areas. I was also not to display large amounts of currency, and was warned to avoid eating/drinking anything that was not factory-wrapped.

As I stood at the edge of the property maintained by my hotel, I almost turned around and went back to my room. I decided that would be boring and cowardly (though prudent), so I watched for the least-deadly time to cross. Like jumping into a fast-moving river, there was no way to enter traffic "gradually".

The area across the road from my hotel was a "mixed-use" area (as are most places in India, in my limited experience), holding apartments, small shops, street vendors, and, at the end, a school with a large front yard of beaten dirt. Upon crossing the road, I found myself in the most diverse crowd I had ever witnessed – a small drugstore on one corner, a tailor shop on the other, goats, carts carrying tiny idols and trinkets, children chasing each other...

And noise of all types, all around me. That was something I noticed quickly – the noise in Mumbai never stops – constant traffic, Muslim calls to prayer, shouting... I first stopped at the drugstore, to buy some tummy medicine (jet lag messed up my system) and some candy to give away to kids. I was looking for a large group of children – I figured that a white guy shouting "Candy!" would be enough of a clue.

That's how I found the school at the end of the street, with about 60 kids wearing uniforms, playing soccer and cricket on packed earth. Once I shouted "Free candy!", I was besieged by outstretched arms. It got so bad at one point that I could no longer see faces; only brown wrists and hands. In about three minutes, my large supply of candy was all gone, but the hands were still questing. I tried to show the kids my empty hands, but they didn't believe me.

I helplessly turned back toward the other end of the street, leading a parade of perhaps 50 kids. They began to drop off by fives and tens as they figured out that I wasn't immediately going to buy more candy. I tried to explain – that just caused my diminishing retinue to reach their questing hands toward me again.

Back in the mass of humanity once again, I marveled at where & how Indians live. Sidewalks do not exist as walkways; they're most often new home sites. A poor Indian will put up a tarp, held up by four poles, to claim a section of the cement. He'll then purchase a foam mat on which to sleep, plus a skillet, cup, and dish, and housekeeping is established.

The local government will bulldoze such structures from time to time, reported in newspaper stories which voice concern over the local government's harsh treatment of its poor. The previous inhabitants immediately begin to rebuild, and soon the sidewalk is once again impassible to pedestrians.

As I walked back up the street, I spotted on my left a barbershop, in which a young man had just been given a shave with a straight razor. I momentarily considered getting a shave, but then remembered the nonexistent sanitation, and that contracting dengue fever was not on my to-do list for this trip.

I again crossed the busy street, back to my hotel, and decided that I'd experienced enough terror for the first day. No problem – a new nightmare awaited me when I reported to the client's offices the next morning!

My First Class in India

...And I was ill the whole time I was in India

Worlds Away – pt. 2

When the driver came to the door of my hotel to transport me to the client's offices, I didn't quite know what to expect. Yes, I knew that my client was an international conglomerate with production facilities around the globe, and that I'd be teaching 15 other trainers how to use a rapid training development tool designed to work with ERP applications. Their HR Director had heard me teach a "Tips & Tricks" session at an HR conference, and decided that his trainers needed to hear me.

And I'd been told to expect a driver who would be assigned to me all week, for safety & convenience. The office where I'd be training was 25 minutes away from my hotel. Of course, in Mumbai traffic, that could mean it was 5 blocks away. Traffic in Manhattan is <u>nothing</u> compared to Mumbai. There are lane dividers, stop signs, and traffic lights... but no one pays any attention to them. There are also no sidewalks, as I mentioned in pt. 1 of this article.

In any traffic situation, the mix of pedestrians, bicycles, and vehicles is risky; in Mumbai, it's downright life-threatening. Men selling sheets of foam (for bedding), micro-vans carrying 9 adults, motorcycles carrying families of five, and a huge number of compact cars competed for space with a few luxury SUVs and the occasional Rolls-Royce. Most streets were lined with ramshackle dwellings, unless they were lined with street vendors.

Having been warned by several people not to eat anything purchased from a street vendor (I <u>love</u> street food), I resisted, but still had an upset stomach and... let's say, an impatient digestive system, for the entire week. The pink bottle was my very good friend for the duration of my time in India.

When we finally arrived at our destination, I had no idea in which direction my hotel lay. I was very relieved when my driver told me he would pick me up to return to my hotel within 20 minutes of when I called him. Fortunately, the security guard at the client offices had been told to watch for me, and I passed through the metal detector and x-ray units without incident. The Sales rep who was my liaison between the client and my consulting firm led me to the conference room in which the class would be held.

Upon opening the door to the aforementioned conference room, I was immediately struck by its size – I had a walk-in closet that was nearly as large. The wall opposite the door was mirrored, which didn't make the room feel any bigger, just more crowded. The room contained 15 trainees, the local head of HR, two IT techs, my company liaison, and me. Plus, every 20 minutes, two food-service attendants came in with coffee, tea, and snacks.

The technicians worked for another hour, trying to make the application behave properly. At that point, I decided I could wait no longer, and began to introduce myself and the course, while the techs continued to work. I could already tell it was going to be a loooong week.

Mercifully, after 30 minutes of trying to teach while the IT technicians worked fruitlessly, they gave up for the day, and the situation became a bit less chaotic. I was able to deliver my standard "geography lesson", pointing out how the main screens were laid out, and talking a bit about what each link/button did. By the end of the day, I was still unsure that my trainees understood much that I had said, because Indians are taught that it is rude to question what a teacher says, even if they have no idea of its meaning.

The next 4 days of training were held in a larger conference room, and we continued to limp along in the application I was attempting to teach them. By the third day of class, just before our first break, one of my trainees, a demure young lady, finally raised her hand shyly and confessed: "Kent... I have a doubt."

This was her way of communicating to me that she had not understood something I had said.

I was thrilled, because the only elements of feedback I had gotten up to that point were vague smiles and the classic Indian nod, which made me think I was teaching an entire class of bobble-head dolls. If you've never witnessed this, it's a bit confusing at first: an Indian will appear to be expressing disagreement, while smiling. But if you watch closely, you'll notice that his/her head is tilting from side to side – this is the

Indian way of expressing: "Yes, everything is peachy, and all is right with whatever you might be saying!".

This young lady expressed confusion with an expression I had repeatedly used, and I had to evaluate how I was communicating with the class – the idioms I was using meant nothing to them, and when the class returned from break, we all got a laugh as I explained my communication snafu. Then I tried to tell a "blonde" joke, and had to explain that a stereotype in America is that blonde women are dumb.

Each afternoon, my driver would be called to return me to my hotel. He would attempt to ask about my day, but his limited command of English meant that our conversations were pretty basic. After a 20-minute drive through hellish traffic, we would pull into the hotel parking lot, where the underside and the trunk of the car would checked for explosive devices. I would drop off my computer bag and head to the hotel restaurant for an excellent (and tremendously expensive) meal.

Breakfasts and dinners at the hotel were sumptuous, though beef was not readily available (since most Hindus revere cows). I had lunch each day in the employee cafeteria of my client, where I ate "Veg" with my trainees, since most of them were strict vegetarians. I also tried to avoid using my left hand while eating, since there's a cultural taboo against that. Indians in the old days used the left hand for... let's say "dealing with the remains of the <u>opposite</u> bodily function".

Next time – Indian beaches, the Hyderabad Tech Center, and meeting a goat.

A small answer to prayer

Worlds Away – pt. 3

On the next-to-last day of my time in Mumbai (before I flew to Hyderabad, in a different state), I determined to walk to a nearby shopping mall, to see what an Indian mall was like. What I discovered was a shopping experience similar to visiting a mall in the USA, except that I had to pass through a metal detector and a cordon of armed guards before entering. I also discovered that I could afford little in this mall more substantial than ice cream (which was amazingly good!). I almost bought a pair of socks for the equivalent of $15 US, but decided against it.

I'm not a "Neiman-Marcus" shopper, instead buying most of my clothes from the Haggar ® factory store, Kohl's, or Marshall's (if I can pry myself away from the kitchen section!). If I'm ever complimented on my clothing, I just tell the truth: "Thank you – my wife dresses me."

After determining that I would not be returning to the USA with an item I purchased from the Indian mall, I made my way back toward my hotel, stopping to watch a group of small boys playing cricket in a walled-off area behind a small house. I understand very little about cricket, but cheered them on anyway when one of them seemed to do something well.

About a block from my hotel, I noticed two young boys feeding the family goat on the sidewalk. I had no doubt that this animal constituted a large part of this family's wealth, and, as I was looking on, the lady of the house came out, smiled broadly at me, and gestured toward the goat. I don't speak Hindi (or any other Indian language), but I finally deduced that she wanted me to meet her goat. She lifted its right front hoof, and I shook it as warmly as I could manage.

After a nice dinner and a restless night (I never got used to the time difference), I concluded my first week of teaching with a short day, awarding my trainees gifts of every conceivable item I could give away. I received, in return:

- A brass elephant
- Indian chocolate drink mix
- Several bookmarks
- A small package of saffron
- A sash for my wife
- Several small, carved wooden animals

- A USB drive carrying the logo of their conglomerate

To show his pride in his country, the Sales rep from my consulting firm who had set up this training took me on a tour around Mumbai, including their strange beach. When I told him I'd like to walk down to the water and dip my feet, just to say that I had, he cautioned me against it. Because the water is so polluted, no one visiting the beach actually touches it – they just hang out, meet friends, and look out at the ocean.

After carting me around the city for a couple of hours, then sharing a seafood dinner with me at a restaurant he recommended, he returned me to my hotel, where I packed my bags and spent another restless night. The next morning, I was on my way to teach another group in Hyderabad, in the Tech Center area of the city. The huge Oracle (owner of the software I usually taught) building stood out from all the others.

Hyderabad has a totally different character from Mumbai. It's not nearly as crowded, and there are lots of "tech workers" – mostly computer folks. There are still beggars, and poverty, but there's an energy to the city – lots of people are "movin' on up" (Yep, just like in *The Jeffersons* theme song).

This week promised to be much easier than my week in Mumbai – in Hyderabad, I was teaching Effective Communications to employees in the India division of the big consulting firm that employed me. They took advantage of the fact that a client was already paying to fly me to India (on Air India – Oh, my!), and snagged me for several days of helping their staff learn to speak and write to a Western audience.

I met amazing folks, including a security guard who insisted on saluting me every morning when I entered our company's offices. My interaction with the India staff and their managers inspired me to develop a course on 'Spotting and Developing Leaders'. I'm certain that several of them have grown into positions of vastly increased responsibility.

Ask for a Blue one!

I'm fascinated by tiny, bright, tropical tree frogs. I love their vivid colors and the tiny suckers that allow them to perch almost anywhere. It's incredible that God designed something so tiny that can still carry out all biological functions. I feel the same way when a hummingbird whizzes by.

I was visiting the Baltimore Aquarium; climbing the winding ramp to view the "non-fish" exhibits. When I got to the "Poison Tree Frog" exhibit, I spent a few minutes watching a green one perch on the front glass wall, then moved on to a display of a red one with black stripes down its back, and a yellow one with white dots. Then I stopped, because the next display contained a blue tree frog – according to the photo on the wall.

Now, I didn't even know they came in blue, but the display looked empty. Since I'd never seen a blue tree frog, I looked intently for it, but to no avail. Someone told me it was hiding behind a rock, but I moved on to the next display. Then I stopped, because I <u>really</u> wanted to see a blue one, and went back to try again – and this time I prayed.

 "God, I've never seen a blue one, and I'd really like to! Thanks." Because I've learned to pray for little things and big things. I don't always get everything I want (Thank you, Lord!), but I've seen some neat "little" prayers answered "Yes!". For instance, when board shorts were all the rage, I saw a wild pair that suited my taste perfectly, but in Medium (certainly not my size).

So I prayed that I'd find a pair just like that in my size. Something prompted me to a particular bin, where I found it almost immediately. Obviously, my Father loves to bless me - with big things and little things, and things I don't even notice! And He even takes care of me when my attitude stinks.

25 years ago, I was a counselor at a boy's home. It was a stressful, low-paying job. Every day (or night), when my 10-hour shift ended, I would stand in front of my 5-gallon aquarium and watch my tropical fish – they helped me relax. One morning, as my day off was about to begin, I was grousing (to myself) that I didn't even have enough money to buy a new guppy.

Apparently, God was listening! In my mail that day was a note from friends back home. This middle-aged man and his 10-year-old son, both of whom were my good friends, had been sharing a soda break, when Matthew remarked that the only thing that would make the experience better was if I were there (back in Texas) to share it with them.

So his dad, Steven, stuck $2 and the note in an envelope. But Matthew had already put a dollar of his own money in the envelope. So Steven just sent me the $3, and told me I should have fun with it. I bought a new guppy that afternoon, and repented.

But, back to the tree frog story. After I prayed, I watched the front glass of the exhibit and waited about 30 seconds – and out from behind a rock popped the coolest bright-blue little critter I have ever seen! Ever since that day, I have kept a framed photo of a blue tree frog on the wall of my house, to remind myself that God hears and answers prayers for small things.

And I remind "my" kids at church (and a few of the youth, as well) to ask Him for big things in their lives as well. I use an object lesson – I'll open a bag of individually-

wrapped candy and tell him/her to put a big hand into the bag and grab as much as they can. Then I quote this verse: "God is able to do exceedingly, abundantly, more than you can ask, or even think!".
Sometimes I'll follow that with a paraphrase of another verse, "If God the Father gave Jesus for you, is there anything good He won't give you?".

For kids who are repeating the "big grab" lesson, I also remind them to ask God for specific things they want Him to do in their lives, or with their lives, or for someone else. Because, if we don't ask God for specifics, how will we know to thank Him for giving us what we asked?

I've learned to pray for big things, little things, and everything in between. Lately, I've been asking Him for the chance to write for a larger audience. My book, out on Amazon, is part of that. It's called 'Thank You, my Friends – the 5-year Plan'.

Because, in the 5 years (since August) that I've lived in East Texas, He has shown that He still has a plan for my life – and it's really cool!

Leading the Parade...

(Note - I wrote these paragraphs for the back of Papa's funeral program)

The last significant thing I said to Papa was a vision God gave me of my Dad leading a procession of people to heaven. Dad led his family, a multitude of parishioners in the United States, and many from other countries he visited in knowing God better. He helped young ministers know how to lead others to know God better, and some of those led others.

In this way, his life was invested in so many other people, sometimes in a long chain reaction. Each of us spends his or her life in some way, investing it in something. My Dad chose to invest in communicating the grace and life of God in the lives of others, and because of that investment, his life led a long parade toward his Rock, his Light, and his Life.

Nothing meant more to Dad than touching the lives of others with the Gospel, and nothing would mean more to those who loved him than to know that this celebration of his life drew others to Jesus. If you are not already in the group of those drawn to Him by the life and words of my Dad, please join us now. Commit your life to God by trusting in Christ to forgive your sin and be in charge from now on. Get in the parade – you'll love where we're going, and you won't regret the trip!

Papa preparing to preach in Russia

The Only Rock Ts

Many years ago, I designed, produced, and sold t-shirts for the Christian youth market. My biggest seller was a play on the slogan of the most popular Rock station in the Dallas area –. Their slogan was "Q102 - Texas <u>Best</u> Rock". My design used the same colors and font, with the words "Jesus - Texas <u>Only</u> Rock". (If you're interested, I ran out of those shirts long ago, but I think I still have a few window stickers left).

I've always loved wearing t-shirts with a message, but I haven't designed any in 20 years – until now. My new "message" t-shirt isn't silk-screened – it's hand-lettered, pretty crudely. In bold colors, and simple lettering, it reads: "Forget Me" (front), Remember Jesus (back).

I've been meaning to produce this t-shirt for months, ever since I first heard *Only Jesus* (by Casting Crowns). Some of the lyrics are: "...*Jesus is the only name to remember | And I – I don't want to leave a legacy / I don't care if they remember me / Only Jesus... | I – I've only got one life to live / I'll let every second count for Him / Only Jesus*"

When I first moved to East TX, alone, broken, and searching for daily hope, I consciously took time to mourn the fact that I was unlikely to ever have kids of my own. The Sipes "family name" is secure, carried on by one of my nephews (and his two wonderful sons), but there will never be a "Kent, Jr." running around.

Part of that sadness was the idea of being forgotten, soon after I'm gone. But everyone except the <u>most</u> famous is eventually forgotten – few people leave a really lasting mark on this world. And I do enjoy the mark I get to leave on the the kids at our church whose lives I get to brighten up. For years, I was the "Candy Man" – dispensing hard candy, hugs, and individual attention to kids from 2-12 (a few adults regularly requested candy, too, because "Mr. Kent always has candy!").

But, as I've written in a few articles, the candy, the welcome, and any other efforts on behalf of "my munchkins" is never about me – they're unlikely to remember, 20 years from now, that it was me who was kind to them. And that's just fine! What I want them to remember is that, when they came to church, a grown-up spoke to them, remembered their names, and saw them as important. And, just maybe, I can help point them to the real Source of everything good.

In my church, we talk about "pouring into" lives. It's another way of saying that we invest in people. We do that because we care about them, and we want them to see the love that really motivates us, so that some of them will turn to Jesus as the only hope. He is "The Only Rock", after all!

So, if you see a big, middle-aged guy walking around in a crudely-lettered t-shirt, it's just my personal "mission statement". It's like the line in an old song from DC Talk (*Jesus Freak*): "*I saw a man with a tat on his big, fat belly / It wriggled around like marmalade jelly / It took me a while to catch what it said / 'Cause I had to match the rhythm of his belly with my head / "Jesus Saves" is what it raved / In a typical tattoo green / He stood on a box in the middle of the city / And he claimed he had a dream*!".

But I'm not <u>about</u> to get a tattoo, and no one wants to see me with my shirt off, anyway. It's the message that matters – not looking cool, not "winning people to my way of life" – just Jesus. He's the answer –

the Truth, Life, and Way. The best thing I can do is to point folks to Him – with my words, with my life... and even with my t-shirt. So, forget me – remember <u>Jesus</u>.

Some of our "Youth Group" from the 1980s – we've changed a bit!

The guy on the left is wearing one of the shirts I designed way back when.

Philistine Art Appreciation

Driving to my Mama's house in Mesquite, I'm always confronted with an incomprehensible piece of "public art". For those of you who don't know about this phenomenon, "public art" usually means a sculpture of some sort erected on city land. The sculpture is usually unrecognizable as "representative of nature", because, apparently, if it can be recognized as, let's say, "a representation of a horse", it's not "art". For a sculpture to be "art", it must look like nothing/no one the average person would recognize ("Oh, yes, that's a bust of Abe Lincoln!"), unless under the influence of mind-altering chemicals.

As a professional traveler (my work takes me around the USA, and occasionally to other countries), I've been repeatedly exposed to public art. Walking between my hotel and workplace in Chicago, I often passed a massive upside-down pyramid, which was supposed to represent the minority struggle for equal rights. And I'm even subjected to public art when *passing through* cities, like the Detroit airport, which uses a tunnel between terminals to simulate storms.

I actually like that "art", although most storms I've encountered never seem to include the color pink, or soothing synthesizer tones. I just hope they don't add sprinklers to simulate rain, or a wind turbine blowing straws through utility poles, as part of a "tornado experience". And, since I'm writing about airport art, the Norfolk, VA airport has extensive displays of photography, collages, sculpture, paintings, murals... But some of them might not really be "art", because I can recognize a few of the elements that make up the pieces ("Ah, that's a railroad freight car displaying colorful graffiti! And that's a ceramic donut!").

One city I visited decided to combine its livestock heritage with modern art by inviting local artists to customize identical bull sculptures, by painting them and adding additional elements (like whimsical hats, beads, blankets...) At least, in that case, I could recognize the underlying animal being portrayed. Another city did the same thing with park benches, but none I saw were wearing hats.

When I lived in Columbia, MO, I loved to take my computer to the public library to do my work (I was a freelance writer at the time). I could sit on the 2nd floor landing and look out the soaring, 3-story front window while I worked. My view was spoiled, though, by a mess of "art". Someone had commissioned a sculptor to create something titled "Joy of Discovery", which apparently, translated into metal. 300 pieces of metal were welded together into an incomprehensible shape resembling in nothing in nature, then painted in bright, cheerful colors.

True "public art" is probably purchased by a committee – no one person could be that stupid. I asked my buddy, Beach, once what made something "art" – he told me that if the right people say "It's art!", then it is. I'm not sure who those "right people" are, but they apparently think that random glops of paint that look as if they were slung onto the canvas by a drunken monkey are very important.

I understand that I am not an "artsy" person, though my university education tried to help me "appreciate" art. Unfortunately, when I took Art Appreciation class in junior college, I was loading trucks for a meat company all night. When I showed up for that 8 AM class, my eyes closed almost immediately after the teacher dimmed the lights to begin the slideshow that was to expose us to the fine art.

The only art I immediately liked was "Western" art; paintings by Frederick Remington. I recently saw a picture of his used as the cover of a Mark Twain book called *Roughing It*, about his experiences in the California Gold Rush as a young man. The painting was of a group of mountain men telling stories around a firepit in a large tent, and it made me imagine the stories those men were telling. If I were ever to purchase a piece of art, it would be that one.

A little bit of "fine art" got through, though – I learned to appreciate Impressionism, the style in which the pictures evoke a particular mood, because they're blurry – but they still look like something I can recognize. The only Impressionist painter whose name I remember is Monet, and I've seen several of his paintings that I like. And I'm fascinated by the images some folks can create with watercolors – I can only make shapeless blots.

The art that's most meaningful to me, though, is that done by people I love. Every few weeks, I'll receive a gift of a "kid picture" – sometimes, I can even tell what it's supposed to be <u>before</u> the kid tells me. Whether I can recognize what the picture depicts or not, these always go on my fridge for a few weeks. And a sun catcher given me by one of my "little friends" (Hi, Vanessa!) has graced my back porch for months.

Two of my wife's paintings are hanging in my home office, because I like them more than she does. And I've been promised a painting by Ms. Sue (my amazing Sunday School teacher) when she's gone from this life. The painting is nice, but what's really important about it is that <u>she</u> created it, and it's part of her home décor. Oh – and the painting is of something I recognize.

So, maybe I'm a Philistine – that's the term "cultured" folks apply to those who don't recognize what they call "fine art". Heck, I regularly create fine art in my kitchen – you should see a pan of my BBQ chicken after the sauce is broiled onto the skin – beautiful!! And when I put away the leftovers (Ha!), you might spot a kid picture on the fridge door – now that's my kind of art!

In my element, working a conference booth

Allow Me to Introduce Myself...

A few years ago, I taught a class of up-and-coming Indian managers how to talk about themselves. I gave them a homework assignment: to do a 5-minute introduction of themselves, including their time with their company, their job title, job responsibilities, major skills, and the sports they either play or watch regularly. Some were better than others, of course, but everyone seemed a bit bemused about the purpose of this exercise.

Then I explained its purpose. All of us, and especially leaders, must speak in public from time to time. This may be in the context of a meeting with a work team, an elevator conversation, or a client presentation. To begin becoming more comfortable speaking, why not practice presenting the subject most of us know best: ourselves?

But I also wanted them to understand what a speaker introduction does for the audience: it establishes the value of the speaker, and gives some insight into his/her "real life". Establishing value is important because listeners judge right away how much energy and attention to devote to a speaker, based on perceived credibility. Insight into the speaker's life gives listeners a chance to find some commonality with him/her, a "hook" to help persuade them to invest in this person.

Of course, too much or inappropriate information can turn off listeners, so it's best to stick to surface information. I often share that my wife is a therapist and that I jog with my dog. Then I show a photo of Purt (my big puppy, overdue for his first grooming), who in this photo looked somewhat like Cujo, but a bit less menacing.

A 5-minute introduction is too long for most situations, but I gave that time threshold to prevent the introductions from being too short to be good practice. And the use I have in mind is a taped self-critique. Trainees are told to write down the bullet points of their introduction, then I will record their presentation, and the group will help them pick out the major issues. Then he/she chooses one "trouble spot" at a time to fix.

Fixing one thing at a time is the approach I was taught in A+ computer maintenance training. And many efficiency experts today advise against multi-tasking, since it seems that when we do more than one thing at once, none is as good as it would have been if we concentrated on it alone. In public speaking, we really can only give attention to one problem area at a time.

For instance, a speaker might choose to first eliminate the use of filler words and phrases (such as "uh", "like", and "you know"). When listening to the recording, he/she would note the number of times fillers occurred. Then he/she would make a new recording of the introduction, concentrating on not using fillers, and listen to the playback, noting how much success had been achieved.

The process would be repeated until fillers were mostly (or totally) eliminated. Then he/she would listen to the new recording, noting another issue, such as volume. As I've written previously, most of us are only used to hearing ourselves from both inside and outside our heads, giving us a false sense of our volume and resonance. Most people aren't nearly as loud (or resonant) as they think they are – that's why hearing their own voices on tape horrifies most people.

Even those who are loud enough overall may have other "volume" issues, such as trailing off at the end of sentences, or poor enunciation. Depending on the audience, other issues might need to be addressed, such as slang. For instance, when speaking to a group in India, I had to choose a different word to express the term "freelancing", because the term had a much narrower meaning there than in the USA.

Maybe you'd like to practice introducing yourself in different situations. It's very necessary in most fields, for the same reasons I mentioned at the beginning of this article – it establishes your credibility and provides an opportunity for connection. And it's a great tool with which to improve your public speaking!

Canoewbies

Calvin and I were new to shooting the rapids on the Guadalupe River in the Texas Hill Country – my brother Kevin (see my *Super Sipes* column) and his friend Tony (our church Youth Leader) had canoed on the river once before, so they were seasoned veterans. At 15, I got to go along because Kev was my big brother, and he was definitely "in charge" on the trip. Of course, he was in charge in lots of situations – leadership is a big part of his nature.

Tony and Kevin were in their early 20s, Calvin was 18, and I was the (very) enthusiastic kid, along for the ride. We had set up camp the night before, right beside the dock – truly a primo spot. Though Kevin and I had been camping lots of times, Tony had only camped once, so he decided to sleep <u>outside</u> the tent. He told us he had never seen a shooting star, and that he was determined to see one that night, even if it meant staying awake all night.

After only 5 minutes of staring into the sky, he saw his first one. In fact, we all enjoyed a spectacular light show that night – there was a meteor shower that lasted about 10 minutes. I was thrilled to be included with my big brother and Tony, sleeping under the stars, even though the ground beneath our sleeping bags was rocky, cold, and slanted downward.

I volunteered to make breakfast for the group the next morning – scrambled eggs and sausage. After a hearty breakfast, we trudged up to the campground canoe rental booth and picked up our life vests. Then we piled in a beat-up, faded blue van for the ride to the put-in point, about 4 miles up-river. After 10 minutes of basic instructions, we slid our canoes into the river and prepared to face our first white water.

Kev and Tony went first, to demonstrate rowing in tandem to navigate the first, tame rapids safely... and promptly turned over. Then they watched, disbelieving, as Calvin and I ignorantly let the current turn us 180 degrees and we went through backward, without a hitch, laughing nervously the whole time. We decided that they must have exaggerated the difficulty of rowing through rapids, and raised our paddles over our heads in victory.

About 10 minutes later, we figured out that our canoe was different from theirs – their seats were flush with the top of the canoe, while ours were set about 6 inches lower. The lower center of gravity was the secret to our success.

The next rapids were much tougher than the first set, with narrow passes between huge boulders. Calvin and I tried to row in a coordinated fashion, but we weren't very good at it – we flipped over right away, and were immediately swimming for our lives. Fortunately, everyone had prepared for the canoes to flip - our towels, sunscreen, and snacks were tied in plastic grocery bags. But this turned out to only keep water <u>in</u> the bags, preventing their contents from drying out.

Besides not drowning as I careened off the huge rocks, I was most concerned with reaching the bag containing my towel and beef jerky. At first, I was a bit dubious about continuing to eat jerky dipped in river water, but I reasoned that I was ingesting large amounts of brown water anyway. Within 30 minutes I was dropping it to the floor of the canoe in between ripping off chunks with my teeth – I had decided to let my immune system protect me from whatever might be in the water.

And I knew there was lots of foreign matter floating in the river, because I put some of it there. Just that morning, Kevin had pointed out to me that the folks swimming near the dock probably didn't appreciate me scrubbing the breakfast pans and dumping the greasy egg remains into the water only 3 feet from them.

I'd like to repeat the trip, with our sons, sons-in-law, etc. – maybe this summer. I'm not sure I can convince Ben to join us – he went to the "Guad" with me and a neighbor kid when he was 14, just before I married his Mom, and it was not a fun experience. We went in August, and I should have remembered that the water level is very low by that time of year. That meant no rapids, and large sections of the river over which we had to "portage" – drag or carry our canoes.

It was also very hot, and Scooter, the other kid, had never been camping, so he had no idea what the vents in the tent were for. He decided he should close them before bedding down the first night, and I awakened at 1 AM, feeling as if I were trying to nap in a sauna. I could hear the wind howling outside the tent, but absolutely no air was moving inside. After re-opening the vent flaps, I was able to get

2 or 3 hours of sleep – perfect preparation for 4 miles of dragging a canoe over mud and rocks!

So... maybe I'll bring my son-in-law, Josh. He and I like to cook, and he's a lot of fun. Kevin and Tony are retired, and they're occasionally in touch with Calvin, who's still working. Kevin might bring one or both of his sons, and Tony can bring a son-in-law or two. I don't know who Calvin might bring, but having him there would certainly bring back some of the fun we had "way back when" – more than 40 years ago.

We may even try to re-create some scenes from the first trip that I captured with my little 126 camera, like Tony sitting in a half-submerged canoe with a goofy grin on his face, or Kevin doing his best Tarzan rope swing, right into Calvin, who does a pretty good stunt version of being knocked from the canoe... or me scrubbing breakfast pans – but not in the river (at least, not if anyone's swimming nearby).

Some of the "art" that decorated my little rent house - album cover from 'Wake the Nations'

Play that Funky Music... Till you Die

Until last week, I had a fluffy white beard. This was the first time I'd ever let it grow for more than 2 weeks – usually, I just look a little "scruffy", but my wife and I agreed that I should avoid shaving (except my neck) until my very difficult assignment in Virginia was over (as a sort of protest). But now that it's over, I'm unemployed, and the beard might not fit the professional appearance I want to convey. And, as my sweetie reminds me, Purt eats a lot of pricey dog food, so the beard had to go.

It may have made me look my age, which might explain why my "little friend" Vanessa said what she did. Vanessa and two of her male cousins (whom I'd only met once) piled in my wife's SUV with me for a run to the donut shop – 3 kids, under the age of 6. One of the boys mentioned that his mom **never** let him go with strangers (I had gotten permission from his grandparents), and I wanted to reassure him that I was a friend of the family. I said, "Vanessa and I have been friends for a long time, right, Vanessa?", to which she replied, "Yes, you are my bestest friend and you will be my friend until you <u>die</u>!".

Well, that's a true statement, but I might have phrased the sentiment differently. As my "little friends" age out of our kid's program and transition to the Youth group, I often remind them that I'm their "friend for life". After all, the Bible says, "Don't forsake a friend, or the friend of your father's". And the relationship changes – we're still not equals, but they can certainly call me "Kent", instead of "Mr. Kent", at that point, and I don't give them orders like children (unless they need them).

I do, however, still give them the opportunity to put a "big hand" into my candy bag – no one ages out of that lesson. Here's how the "Big Hand" lesson goes: I tell a kid to reach a big hand into my bag and come out with as much as he/she can hold. The first time a kid does this, the look on his/her face is wondrous, about like mine the first time I got to eat a whole pizza by myself. Then I tell them, "Every time you reach a big hand into the bag, I want you to remember to ask God for **big things** in your life!".

The next time a kid does the Big Hand grab, I add to the lesson. I ask if he/she remembers what the Big Hand exercise stands for, and remind the kid if necessary. Then I ask what, specifically, he/she wants God to do in, through, or for him/her – I usually get a blank look in response. That's when my sermonette starts: "If you don't ask God for specific things, how will you know when He does it?!?". The 3rd time a kid does the "Big Hand" grab, he/she had better know that it stands for "big & specific", and be ready to tell Mr. Kent their prayer request.

I have my own stories of big, specific things I've asked God for, like the time I was enrolling in Bible College and needed a part-time job that would allow me to study while I worked. I found a job managing parking lots for a large hospital complex, which gave me plenty of time to study, pray, play the guitar (I still stink at it), and have picnics with my buddy, "Yo, Pete".

Yo Pete drove a catering truck, which meant that he had a nearly unlimited supply of snacks and sodas. He would pull into the lot I was managing, and we'd sit on the grass eating Hostess Cupcakes, root beer, Doritos, beef sticks, powdered-sugar

300

donuts... it's no wonder Yo Pete had a "Dunlap" belly in his 20's, and I wasn't far behind him. I called him "Yo, Pete" because, back in the day, he could only be contacted via voice pager (way before cell phones were common). To let him know who was calling, I always prefaced my messages with the greeting, "Yo, Pete!".

As I've written (*Dream Car*, from my book *Thank You, my Friends – the 5-year Plan*), "Yo, Pete" had the gift of "automotive infallibility", and could fix any car/truck problem. He may not have actually been able to fix *any* vehicle problem, but he certainly did fix the ones I encountered, and, compared to my own automotive skills, he certainly seemed super-human. I, on the other hand, once attempted to change my own brake pads, and managed to put them on *backward* (something automotive professionals have since told me is impossible).

I've lost touch with this friend over the years, as I moved from Texas to Arkansas, then back to Texas, married, moved to Missouri, moved to Indiana, then divorced and back to Texas – whew! I need to contact my friend, "Beach", to find out if he has contact info for "Yo, Pete". Good thing I lost the white beard – neither of them might have recognized me!.

PS – I've recently added another "candy lesson". If a kid is wearing cargo pants (or shorts, since we're in Texas), I offer to fill up a cargo pocket with candy (that's what those pockets are for, after all!). Then I tell the munchkin that Jesus wants to fill up his/her life in just the same way, and that he/she should ask for <u>everything</u> He wants to give them!

The boys take a nap – and this is why we can't have nice things...

You Can't Always Get what You Want

As an American, I hold the firm belief that money can accomplish anything – if the Waffle House menu doesn't show a 3-egg breakfast, I just tell the server what I want, and he/she brings me the meal I requested, then charges me the correct amount. When I need work done around our property (and have zero construction/maintenance skills), I tell one of my skilled friends what we need done, he tells me about what it will cost, and we get it done.

But, occasionally, dollars just don't do the trick. Many years ago, my best friend "Beach" (a graphic artist) and I decided to launch a t-shirt business. I had some ideas for designs that would appeal to the only demographic group I understood: Evangelical Youth. Our 1st design was pretty simple: we "adapted" a radio station logo that read "Q102 – Texas Best Rock!" to say: "Jesus – Texas Only Rock!", using the same colors, font, etc. We sold a few thousand of them over a period of four years.

We didn't make very good business partners, though, because my vision always differed with his execution, so we decided that I would simply hire Beach to produce the art for my designs. That way, I would get exactly what I wanted, and our friendship wouldn't suffer. So, did I get "exactly what I wanted"? – Ha!

Here's how our business relationship worked: I would describe the picture I saw in my head, possibly accompanied by a pitiful stick-figure drawing. Beach would attempt to interpret my idea, according to "graphic art guidelines" he'd been taught. I would ask him to toss out the "art rules" and just draw what I described. He would change the design slightly, to something *else* I didn't want, but slightly less so.

I would attempt to clarify my vision for the design, and he would counter that the design could not be drawn that way. I would wave money at him in frustration ("I'm paying you – why won't you just draw what I want?!?"). He would say it was impossible, and I would give up, just to stop spending my money and get another design into production.

One example: we produced a "Jesus Radical" shirt that featured a version of the "Black Power" fist icon on the front and three exclamation marks on the back. I asked that Beach use *my* right fist (I have pretty big hands) as a model, then he proceeded to draw something that looked like an arthritic monkey paw. I objected – "Look! Just draw an outline of my fist – see?!?", and he drew another monkey paw. I gave up.

I encountered something like this in central Mexico once, near Delicias, Chihuahua. I was the translator on a mission trip, and we were building a cinder-block structure for a congregation that couldn't do it on their own. One day, we left the jobsite at about 11 AM to try to rent a gas welder. But it didn't matter how many $$ I waved, the guys staffing the tool rental businesses weren't about to interrupt their siestas – from beneath sombreros, one after another told us "Mas tarde" – "Come back later, gringos" - with no **real** indication of what time that meant.

To me, this was unimaginable, but that's only because I've grown up in the USA, where "money talks". I imagine that money talks in Chihuahua, too, just not very loudly at certain times of day (so as not to awaken anyone).

Our quest to rent a welder was carried out in a pickup truck driven by a member of the congregation we were serving, and I wondered why he kept bumping the curb at each intersection. I finally figured out that the truck had no brakes – bumping the curb was the only way he stopped. I was pretty scared, but I decided that God probably hadn't brought me to MEX to die, and prayed that He'd remember I was there on His business.

Then our hosts coasted to a stop at a roadside stand to purchase some tacos for our lunch. They were delicious, but I wondered about the sanitary practices involved in the taco prep, and what kind of road kill might be involved. However, one of the lessons drilled into our heads before leaving on the mission trip was to "eat what's set before you". So I prayed, ate, and thanked our hosts. That was probably the best meal I got all week.

I learned a lot that week – I learned that the rules I grew up with weren't the **only** possibilities, that different life situations produced different priorities, and that money isn't always the answer. And I learned that my friendship with Beach is more important than getting the design I saw in my head, even if I'm paying. And I learned that if I ever design another t-shirt, I should just buy art off the Internet.

One of my hosts in Hyderabad, India – they took me on a boat ride to see a giant idol

*A bike trail in Indiana, reminding me that
the road always curves*

Darling, it's Better, Down Where it's Wetter*

Back in the 1980s, I worked at a boy's ranch in Arkansas. The setting was beautiful, but the work was often stressful, and we made very little money. In fact, I remember being delighted when we once received two boxes of a dead man's clothes, donated by his family. It turned out I was the only person among our staff or students whom the clothes fit.

I got a nifty pair of bib overalls, which began my "hillbilly" look (I also avoided shaving anything but my neck for weeks at a time – but no one noticed). A few people noticed my hair, which fell below my collar in back, and quite concerned my niece (who was 9 years old at the time): "Mama, he's got a ponytail! But he's a boy!! But we love him anyway, right?".

After getting off-shift at 10:30 PM, my usual means of relaxation was to watch the fish in my tiny 5-gallon aquarium. I usually had a few striking fantail guppies, maybe a glass catfish, some Neon Tetras, and maybe a Betta. My fish assortment changed frequently, because I couldn't keep a fish alive for more than a week. I cleaned the tank, checked the pH, didn't overfeed – no matter – they all died.

At one point, I got tired of buying new fish. I happened to be exploring a creek on the Ranch property one day, and noticed that the many crawdads living there didn't seem to care that all manner of used motor oil, grass clippings, and cow poop ran in their water – they survived just fine. I got an idea – why not add a crawdad or two to my tropical tank, just to jazz things up a bit?

The tank now had an added dimension – fancy little fish swimming peacefully above, a crawdad skittering below. Then, on the second day, I noticed that one of my guppies was gone. I decided that I must have miscounted my fish, until the next day when my trio of neon tetras was now a solo act.

My pleas for the denizens of the aquarium to live peaceably ("Can't we all just get along?!?") went unheeded – the predator I had added was making meals of my cute fish – as if I weren't killing them quickly enough! I fished the crawdad out of the tank and returned him to the creek.

I can imagine the story he told the other crawdads: "I was in a box of warm water, with delicious fish swimming right above me, just waiting for me to choose which one I wanted to snag for my next meal, and nothing ever tried to eat me! There was a bright light above me, and a giant, benevolent face beamed at me – I think I went to Heaven for two days!".

My next fish story involved two Bettas – also called "Siamese Fighting Fish". As you might know, two of these magnificent fish in the same tank will supposedly fight until one of them is bedraggled and tired, or dead. Please keep in mind that I was in my mid-twenties when I tell you that I tried this with a pair of Bettas. I kept one in the aquarium and the other in a tiny Betta bowl.

When I felt ready to see a gladiator match, I moved the bowl-dweller to the aquarium, and braced myself for the melee. What happened was: nothing. Each Betta just hung motionless, occasionally moving a graceful fin to maintain its position in the tank. If I eased them closer together, they just continued to hang out, each seemingly unaware of the other's presence.

Apparently, Walmart sells defective Bettas. Or maybe the water was too warm, and they were both convinced they were in a large Jacuzzi. There <u>were</u> constant bubbles, after all! Or maybe they won't fight when anyone's looking... or maybe these two were Betta runway models, loathe to damage their pretty fins.

Given the fact that some folks in today's politically-correct society insist on delving into each person's history; 30, 40, or even 80 years back, I may be sent to "re-education" for my Betta experiment. Maybe I'll be forced to join an animal cruelty counseling group with Michael Vick. It's a good thing my wife is a Therapist – maybe I can just get help from <u>her</u> for my despicable act – from 30 years ago.

I think I've matured since then – that's one of the benefits I've gained... at the cost of back pain, stiffness, gray hair, diminished vision & hearing, etc. Maybe there's a statute of limitations on "Fish Fighting", and the authorities (SPCA?) won't come after me. I'd hate to have to go into hiding or change my name this late in life! And I promise that I'll never again attempt to incite Betta Combat.

From 'Under the Sea', a song from 'The Little Mermaid' – really!

One of the reasons I know I'm His favorite

Yes, I am His Favorite...

The truth must be known – God loves everyone, but I'm His <u>favorite</u>. How do I know? It's the way He treats me. Just look at how many things He made that give me joy:

1. Hummingbirds – tiny, bright, fast, and fierce (to each other)

2. Bettas (AKA Siamese Fighting Fish) – also small, bright, and fierce (but only to other Bettas)

3. Tree Frogs – (see 'Ask for a Blue One!) tiny, bright and slimy (slime is their sunscreen)

4. Lions – my favorite symbol for Jesus is "The Lion of Judah" – majestic, powerful, and beautiful

5. Pansies – especially the deep purple ones

6. Honeysuckle - I'm always surprised and delighted to catch a whiff of this perfume on a spring breeze!

7. Pine trees - Summer is the time for pine trees to throw their aroma out into the air. Part of what makes Texas in August worthwhile is that thick, heavy scent.

8. Coffee – I'm a coffee nerd, and can talk about it like oenophiles discuss their favorite vintages of Red, White, and Rose. I love the smell and I get pretty excited about my favorite varieties of single-origin beans (like Sumatra or Ethiopian Yirgacheffe).

9. Peach Jolly Rancher kisses – these are hard to find today, but they're the best hard candy I've ever tasted. They even have the "bite" of acid, just like a really ripe peach. And they seem to have disappeared from shelves (see my article 'Money Talks – but Not Very Loudly').

10. "Black" Gospel music – sorry, we White folks just can't do that right. I learned this the first time I heard a Gringo choir try to perform the Andre Crouch classic 'Soon and Very Soon'. It was truly painful, and a bit

317

embarrassing. Right now, I'm listening to Kirk Franklin & The Family perform 'Hosanna Forever', and it's doing much more to wake me up than my morning coffee – Whew!!

But, more than the *things* He's made, I'm thrilled that He gave me such a capacity to laugh, and so many things to laugh at. Someone once made fun of me for being "easily amused", but I don't see that as a <u>bad</u> thing. To me, that just means that I'm often amused, and frequently delighted! I'm delighted by:

1. My big, sloppy dog, Purt. He knocks over small items with his long, heavy tail, he tracks in dirt, he steals cookies (and meat) from the counter... and he's full of love.

2. "My kids" – when working with them, I <u>so</u> often laugh out loud. A couple of weeks ago, the kids were lined up by class to play a relay game, when one of the youngest boys got bored and began "swimming" on the polished gym floor. He was immediately joined by two others. This was partly my

318

fault, because I laughed so hard at the first one, and they do <u>love</u> adult attention.

3. Over-the-top humor. Abbott & Costello's 'Who's on First' is a classic example. By the time Lou Costello starts to go crazy with frustration, I'm laughing so hard I can't see. The same thing happens with some scenes from Jim Carrey movies ('Liar, Liar', when he tries to write "The pen is green", but can't) or my favorite stand-up comic, Brian Regan (check out his bit about a hotel clerk trying to find his reservation under a different name).

4. I could name many more reasons why I know I'm His favorite, but the biggest one is that He kept after me when I tried to resist His call, and He keeps working in & through my life – it's amazing! He's blessed my life more than I could imagine – really, "He is able to do exceedingly, abundantly more than I can ask, or even think."

So, yep – it's me – I'm the favorite. I'm special and infinitely valuable, with a wealth of backup, perks, and gifts. I am an adopted Son of God, with Jesus as my big brother. My future is so bright (I gotta wear shades! – 80s reference), and shame from my past is gone, gone, gone. I'm terribly important, and to mess with me requires permission from my Big Daddy.

I'm truly something else.

But, here's a secret – **you're** His favorite, too, entirely as much as me. Only God has that capacity, for love to be undiminished by more than one primary focus.

Enjoy!

Made in the USA
Lexington, KY
04 December 2019

58103060R00202